What the Critics are Saying about H.J. Ralles' Novels

Keeper of the Kingdom

"Aimed at young adults, this is ingenious enough to appeal powerfully to adults who wonder how far this entire computer age can go. Ralles knows how to pace her story—the action moves in sharp chase-and-destroy scenes as Commanders hunt down the dangerous young boy. The pages literally brim with action and computer possibilities and discoveries. The characters are memorable, particularly the very human 101. And that ending . . . is brilliant. A compelling read from exciting beginning to just as exciting ending." *The Book Reader*

"*Keeper of the Kingdom* is a must read for children interested in computers and computer games. From the first page to the last there is no relief from the suspense and tension. H.J. Ralles has captivated anyone with a fascination for computer games, and has found a way to connect computer-literate children to reading." **JoAn Martin,** *Review of Texas Books*

"*Keeper of the Kingdom* is a fun read for younger readers as well as adults. It embodies one lesson for us all. Never, ever, let your computer do all your thinking!" **Jo Rogers,** *Myshelf.com*

"Kids will be drawn into this timely sci-fi adventure about a boy who mysteriously becomes a character in his own computer game. The intriguing plot and growing suspense will hold their attention all the way through to the book's provocative ending." **Carol Dengle,** *Dallas Public Library*

"This zoom-paced sci-fi adventure, set in the kingdom of Zaul, is a literary version of every kid's dream of a computer game. *Keeper of the Kingdom* may be touted for youngsters from 9 to 13, but I'll bet you my Spiderman ring that it will be a "sleeper" for adults as well." **Johanna Brewer,** *Plano Star Courier*

"As in any good video game the PG-rated action is unrelenting, and the good guys never give up. *Keeper of the Kingdom* could be made easily into an adequate Nickelodeon-style kids' movie." *VOYA Magazine*

Darok 9

"Darok 9 is an exciting post-apocalyptic story about the Earth's last survivors, barely enduring on the harsh surface of the moon . . . An enjoyable and recommended novel for science fiction enthusiasts." *The Midwest Book Review*

"Ralles holds us to the end in her tension-filled suspense. We read on to see what surprising events her interesting characters initiate. The scientific jargon and technology does not interfere with the action-filled story which any person can follow even if less versed in the science fiction aspects." **JoAn Martin,** *Review of Texas Books*

"Darok 9 has the excitement of a computer game, put into a book, that parents and teachers will love to see in the hands of their children." **Linda Wills,** *Rockwall County News*

"*Darok 9* is another wonderful science fiction book for young adults by H.J. Ralles, author of *Keeper of the Kingdom*. Filled with nonstop action and suspense, it tells the story of a young scientist, Hank Havard, and his quest to keep his big discovery out of enemy hands. The Language in this book is clean, as it was in *Keeper of the Kingdom*, something I found refreshing. Also, the message that violence doesn't pay is strong. The characters are believable, and the plot is solid. Darok 9 is a can't-put-it-down, go-away-and-let-me-read science fiction thriller, sure to please any reader of any age!" **Jo Rogers,** *Myshelf.com*

"From the first page, the pace of the book is fast and always keeps the reader interested. Young adults will love the suspense that builds and builds as Hank and Will try to avoid being captured." **Conan Tigard,** *Book Browser.com*

"Darok 9 certainly can hold its own in the adult world. This very entertaining book is hard to put down . . . Filled with action and surprises around every bend." **Kelly Hoffman,** *Slacker's Sci-Fi Source*

Keeper of the Realm

With best wishes,

H. J. Rath

Keeper of the Realm

By

H.J. Ralles

Top Publications, Ltd.
Dallas, Texas

KEEPER OF THE REALM

A Top Publications Paperback

First Edition
12221 Merit Drive, Suite 750
Dallas, Texas 75251

ISBN#: 1-929976-21-6
Library of Congress 2002114601

Printed in the United States of America

For

Malcolm

with whom I'll always walk into the future

Acknowledgments

I would like to thank the following people: Malcolm, Richard and Edward my most patient and faithful supporters; Carolyn Williamson and Brenda Quinn, whose editing added so much to this book; Bill Manchee, Lisa Korth and all at Top Publications, who are truly author-friendly; Mark Walker of Ocean's Window, for your valuable information about diving; The Plano Writers, whose honest opinions are always appreciated; Laura Hart of Motophoto, Plano, for great publicity photographs; and my family and friends for their encouragement.

The Realm of Karn

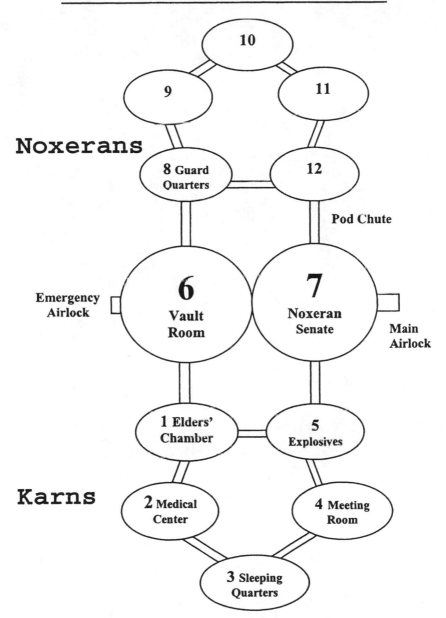

Noxerans

10

9   11

8 Guard Quarters   12

Pod Chute

Emergency Airlock

6 Vault Room   **7** Noxeran Senate

Main Airlock

1 Elders' Chamber   **5** Explosives

Karns

2 Medical Center   4 Meeting Room

3 Sleeping Quarters

Chapter 1

"Someone help me, please!" Matt yelled.

A vibrant blue ball of light flashed past his head. Matt ignored the warning and continued to run. There was no time to rest. Every yard he put between himself and the Cybergons could make the difference between whether he lived or died.

A second shot sped past, perilously close. He fell to the floor and covered his ears as the shimmering sphere struck the wall and exploded with an almighty boom.

Before the smoke cleared, Matt struggled to his feet and shook the splintered fragments of plaster from his blond hair.

"The Forbidden Hall—I must find the Forbidden Hall. It's my only hope."

Matt raced down the corridor looking for the distinctive curved entrance that he remembered seeing in his computer game. He dived through an archway as a third ball whizzed by, and the roof behind him exploded. The force of the blast sent him spinning across the cold floor tiles. A cloud of dust surged at him, stinging his eyes and attacking his lungs.

Coughing and spluttering, he picked himself up a second time and staggered blindly forward into a swirling mass of creamy-colored gases. The vapor billowed from vents in the floor, filling the air with a vile, sulfurous stench and making his blue eyes water. He could hardly breathe. Desperate for air, Matt cupped his hand over his nose and mouth and took short rasping breaths.

A bright light shone through the haze, drawing him toward its brilliance. He strained to focus through the settling dust and found the strength to stagger a few more feet. The clouds began to disperse, and a wave of fresh air enticed him further. He looked for the staircase to the lower level that he had used once before, but it wasn't there.

This isn't the Forbidden Hall, he thought as the air cleared. *Where am I?*

Not believing what he was seeing, he squeezed his eyelids closed and then opened them slowly, but he remained in the same place. He saw none of Zaul's familiar white walls or angular steel girders, nor any silver ceiling pipes or huge floor grids. Matt beat the palm of his hand against his forehead in frustration. Had he leaped through a different archway by mistake?

"Which sector of Zaul am I in?" he questioned in a hoarse voice while frantically scouring the area for Cybergons. None were in sight.

Relieved, but with his heart still racing furiously, Matt took a few seconds to survey a very different environment. He stared ahead. Dozens of powerful neon lights lit the metallic tube-like corridor. It was as if he were inside a huge metal drain. On the curved sides were large red letters—not the strange symbols he had seen on the Cybergons' computers. He traced the words 'Area 5 – DANGER' with his index finger. Then the reality dawned on him. His stomach churned. He felt hot around his neck as panic set in.

"This isn't a different sector—this isn't even Zaul! Where

am I?" he shouted. *Where am I? Where am I?* his voice echoed.

A hand clutched his right shoulder. Matt had been so transfixed by his new surroundings that he hadn't heard anyone approach. He froze. A chill ran from his neck through every bone to his waist as the fingers tightened and pressed down on his collarbone.

"Zaul? I do not know of such a place." A deep voice stressed every syllable. "This is Karn. Please present your identification chip."

Matt held his breath as he twisted slowly around to face the owner of the large hand. The stilted baritone voice did not seem to belong to the tall athletic figure who looked down at him. Dressed in black from head to foot, the man had muscular arms that bulged beneath the thin material of his zippered top. The young man's skin had a metallic golden sheen, which glistened as he turned his head. He had no imperfections—no moles, scars, or blemishes on his face—but on each side of his thick neck were three red parallel markings. Matt swallowed hard. His throat felt dry and tight. Was his captor human?

"Identification chip?" stuttered Matt.

"You are in Area 5. Do you have clearance?"

Matt stared blankly up at his captor. "Area 5? I'm sorry. I didn't realize . . . it was a mistake."

"You will please come with me," said the young man, tightening his grasp closer to Matt's neck. His captor displayed no weapon and had even used the word *please*, but Matt felt threatened enough to accompany him without question. A sliding door, which curved in line with the side of the tunnel-like corridor, opened quietly as they approached.

"Please descend."

The man pointed to a set of sharply winding stairs.

Matt went first with his captor right behind. The hallway at the bottom was dimly lit, leading only into a confined elliptical chamber. Matt hesitated at the entrance and then, realizing that he had no alternative, stepped slowly into the enclosure. The door slid closed, trapping them both in the claustrophobic surroundings.

Six padded seats, fixed in pairs, dominated the center of the small room. Matt was ushered to the front row and ordered to sit down. Without a word, the man leaned over Matt and roughly pushed the boy's arms through two shoulder straps, anchoring them together with a metal fastener across his chest.

"This is for your safety during our journey," he informed.

Matt's eyes focused on the man's leather belt, which separated his long-sleeved top and skin-tight pants. Elaborately engraved on an enormous silver buckle was the letter 'S'. He looked up at his captor's face as the man adjusted the tightness of the harness. His dark sparkling eyes exuded warmth, but his jet-black unkempt hair and austere facial expression made Matt shudder.

Matt wanted to ask many questions, but he had a feeling that this individual who used so few words would not answer them. He diverted his attention to the enormous glass windows surrounding him. Even the ceiling appeared to be transparent, but Matt could see nothing. It was black and ghostly beyond the thick windowpanes.

"The pod will reach Area 4 in five minutes," said the man

with the expressionless face, clipping himself into the seat alongside Matt. "Be prepared for some initial discomfort."

Matt braced himself, unsure what to expect. He figured that perhaps they were in some kind of elevator or transportation device, but he felt no movement up or down.

Suddenly, a loud rush of air engulfed the chamber, and the pod shot forward. Intense pressure pushed Matt deep into the back of his seat as they sped along, giving him both the exhilaration of a theme-park ride and the fear of the unknown. His neck felt as though it might snap with the tremendous force, and momentarily, he had no feeling in his fingertips. Then, as quickly as it had begun, the pressure subsided, and the pod was propelled out of the darkness and into a clear tunnel. Their speed slowed considerably, enabling Matt to take in the view through the windows on either side.

"We're underwater!" he gasped.

"Karn is exactly three hundred feet below sea level," replied his captor.

Matt leaned as far forward as the belt allowed. It seemed as though he were staring into an enormous aquarium. The scenery was breathtaking. He saw vibrant pinks and oranges of coral beds and iridescent colors of unusual fish. He was dazzled by the brightness of the huge underwater lights that illuminated the coral reef. Small dark shapes shot past the pod, and then the more recognizable forms of six-to eight-foot bull sharks.

Without warning the penetrating eyes of a giant eel glared through the glass. As the lengthy body slithered past the window, Matt threw himself back into his seat, shaking with shock. The pod continued to lose speed and rode gently into some kind of dock, quietly connecting with the propelling mechanism at the other end of the tunnel. The windows of the cramped enclosure turned black, and once again, Matt felt as if he were sealed inside an eerie tomb.

A high-pitched tone accompanied the opening of the doors. The man pulled Matt to his feet and pushed him gently forward toward the exit. Matt was faced with another winding set of stairs back to an upper level. He began the climb, his captor close on his heels. At the top, an illuminated metal tunnel, similar to the one in Area 5, stretched as far as he could see.

Matt's shoes reverberated on the floor, which was made of sections of metal mesh suspended across the width of the tunnel. Through the tiny gaps in the latticework beneath his feet, he could see thick silver pipes. Flexible black cables intertwined with the pipes at various points. The curved walls of the corridor were monotonous—highly polished with only a few printed signs to distinguish the first ten feet from the last.

Several similarly dressed individuals passed by. They all glanced in Matt's direction, but walked past without so much as a question. Each man was clothed in black from head to toe with large slip-on shoes, a chunky belt, and no sign of a weapon. Their facial features were different, but each individual possessed the same shiny gold-tinged skin and similar markings on the neck. After his encounter with the Cybergons in Zaul, the thought of being held captive by another race of androids made Matt very nervous.

At the end the tunnel divided. Matt followed silently down

one of the many forks and through a single sliding door into a well-lit windowless room. Splashes of orange in several abstract paintings echoed the warm orange tones of the walls. A wide bed with a yellow covering was molded into the far corner. At one end of the bed a soft pillow and a folded rectangle of silver cloth were stacked neatly.

Matt felt hot. He was unsure whether the temperature of the room was higher than that of the tunnels or if he was sweating with nerves. Or perhaps the bright colors of the room made him feel warmer. He removed his jacket and stood in the center, waiting. *Waiting for what?* he wondered.

"Rest here, please. You will be seen later."

"Seen?" questioned Matt.

His guide didn't answer, but departed through the only exit. The door slid closed. The silence in the room was haunting. No sound of voices or appliances—just an eerie stillness.

Matt kicked off his Nikes, dumped his coat over the back of the tubular chair in the corner of the room, and clambered onto the bed. He curled his arms around his knees and rocked back and forth, sick with worry. Only hours earlier he had thought he would be leaving Zaul and returning home. Instead, he was here—somewhere called Karn.

He bent his head in dismay, fighting back tears. "Home," he muttered. "How I miss home. How *do* I get home?"

He dared not think about whether time stood still during his mysterious travels. Was his mother even aware that he was missing? *Bet she's frantic.*

Tears formed in the corners of his eyes. Matt slapped his cheeks hard, hoping he might awaken from some terrible dream, but the room seemed even hotter. "Matthew Hammond, pull yourself together," he admonished himself.

He wiped the sweat off his forehead with the bottom of his T-shirt and lay back on the bed feeling utterly miserable.

* * * * *

Matt became aware of the presence of someone else in the room. He opened his eyes a crack and tried to focus. An older person peered down at him. The short gray hair glinted under the bright ceiling lights, and the pale green eyes showed familiar warmth.

"Matt, my boy! It *is* you!"

"Varl?" questioned Matt, propping himself up on an elbow. Opening his eyes, Matt recognized the elderly scientist and drew a sigh of relief. "Am I ever glad to see you!"

"Likewise," said Varl, extending his long bony fingers. He grabbed Matt's hand and helped him sit upright on the bed.

A thin boy with unkempt hair stepped forward from the shadows in the corner of the room.

"Targon, my friend from Zaul! You're here too!" shouted Matt with glee.

"Hello, Matt from 2010. Sleeping again?" he teased, playfully thumping Matt on the back. "Perhaps your computer can explain what we're all doing here!"

"Or, even better, where we are and what time period this is," added Varl in a serious tone of voice.

"Computer?" questioned Matt. "Zang it! My laptop! I'd forgotten I had it."

Varl smiled at his choice of words. "I'm pleased to see you remember some vocabulary from Zaul."

"Where could it be?" asked Matt, ignoring his comment.

"You put the circular thing in the slot and pressed those white buttons the last time we saw you," replied Targon.

"I think you've forgotten the computer language I taught you," said Matt. "It was called a *CD-ROM*. And, yes, I was typing in the final commands on the *keys*, because I thought I had finished the *Keeper of the Kingdom* game."

Varl's face lit with excitement. "You were expecting to get back to your own time. I don't suppose we're back in 2010 and this is your home?"

Matt shook his head. "Sorry to disappoint you guys, but this is definitely *not* my home and probably not my time."

"Well then, my boy, I certainly hope your computer is somewhere about," said Varl, his hopes dashed.

"So do I—or I'll never get out of this computer game and back home."

Varl shook his head. "You still maintain we're in your computer game, eh?"

"You said you were a scientist, Varl, and therefore, you believed anything was possible," Matt reminded him.

"True, but I always wondered if you were really a time traveler. Now I'm more convinced. It seems that on this trip you have brought us along, too!"

Matt sighed. "I'm *not* a time traveler, honestly. Right now, I've no idea how I got here and even less of an idea how you came with me. I'm just as confused as you are, and to be honest, I'm *really* missing my home! A week in Zaul with you guys was bad enough—no offense—but now, I find

I'm *here!*"

"Where *is* here?" asked Targon. He turned his back to Matt and ran his index finger along the frame of one of the abstract paintings.

"Karn, I've been told."

"Well then, you've been told more than we have," added Varl. "And where exactly is Karn in relation to Zaul?"

Matt shrugged. "Sorry, but I've no idea. I wasn't told anything else. If I could find my laptop . . ."

"So, how long have you been here?" Varl propped himself against the bed.

"A couple of hours, I guess. One minute I was with you in Zaul, the next I was right here. Without my laptop I'm sunk!"

Targon groaned at the play on words, and Matt forced a smile.

"I think we all are, literally," said Varl, trying to find something humorous about their situation. "This underwater paradise is mighty strange."

"Believe me, this place is no stranger than Zaul," said Matt. "So, how did you get here?"

"Presumably, the same way as you. Targon and I suddenly found ourselves in some glaringly bright corridor and were escorted here by a very untalkative individual. Before that, the last thing I remember is sitting in a room in Zaul and seeing the horrified look on your face when your computer showed the program-error warning. You and I both knew that your game information wouldn't be saved if the computer shut down. I guessed that you thought you'd be starting *Keeper of the Kingdom* over again."

"And that's what I don't get," said Matt, raising the palms of his hands upward. "*I did* start my game again."

"You did?" said Targon.

"Well, just briefly. I found myself running from the Cybergons all over again. I looked for the Forbidden Hall—like I did the first time I landed in Zaul before you rescued me. Only something weird must have happened—because when I dived through the same archway, I ended up here instead."

Varl scratched his stubbly chin as he contemplated Matt's explanation. "I'll soon have a beard like Dorin," he grumbled.

"Oh, no . . . " Targon lamented. "We'd forgotten about Dorin."

"You don't suppose Dorin might also be somewhere in Karn?" said Matt, alarmed. "There *were* four of us in the room—*his* room—when I entered the final commands of my computer game."

Varl continued to scratch his chin as if it irritated him immensely. "It would make more sense for Dorin to be here than for him to have been left behind in Zaul. He was sitting closer to you than Targon. If I remember correctly, Dorin actually had his hands on the lid of your laptop."

"Then why isn't he with us?" asked Targon.

Matt jumped down from the bed and found his shoes. "Perhaps he's here in Karn, but hasn't been found yet. Perhaps he's still in Zaul. Who knows?"

Varl frowned. "So, Matt, what do you make of our situation?"

"You're the scientist, Varl. I was hoping you could tell

me!"

"Sorry, but I'm out of ideas. Your laptop holds the answers."

"Where do you suggest we look for it?" asked Targon.

"For now, nowhere." Varl sat down heavily on the chair. He raised an eyebrow. "I would say that we're at the mercy of whoever has chosen to hold us captive."

"I'm sure we could find our way out of here and back to the place where I came into Karn," said Matt, tying his laces hurriedly. "The corridors weren't exactly busy—we might get lucky." He walked toward the door.

Targon groaned. "You won't be going anywhere. I've already tried the door, and it won't budge."

"You're not seriously suggesting that we just wait here to see what they do with us?" said Matt, glowering at them both. "Neither of you would have waited for the Cybergons to return in Zaul!"

"Look around you, my boy," said Varl. "There's nothing here. Without tools, and a basic understanding of what we're dealing with in the way of technology, I don't see that we have any other choice!"

Chapter 2

The locking mechanism clicked. Matt faced the opening door, anxiously awaiting his fate. Varl moved between the boys and curled his arms tightly around their shoulders. Matt looked at him for reassurance as the door smoothly slid back into the wall.

Instead of the expected muscular, unresponsive male, a slim girl with coal-black, waist-length hair stepped into the room. She wore tight pants and a sparkling golden tunic, which matched her shimmering skin. Matt felt slightly relieved until he noticed three parallel red marks on either side of her neck. His eyes were then drawn to her enormous feet clad in hefty black boots. They seemed totally out of proportion with the rest of her delicate features.

"Welcome to the Realm of Karn. My name is Keela."

Matt frowned. *Did she say Realm of Karn?* He remembered Mrs. Tanyard's eighth-grade language arts class. *A realm is another word for kingdom. Could I still be playing my computer game?*

"You must all be requiring nourishment," said Keela. Her voice was gentle and her words precisely spoken. "If you would like to follow me, your needs will be met."

Targon smiled at the girl. "Food, at last," he said.

Matt was also hungry. The fear he'd felt when the door opened quickly disappeared with the appearance of such a young friendly face. He guessed that he and the girl were the same age.

Varl still looked apprehensive, but he said nothing and left the room after Targon. Matt wondered if he would be given more of the tasteless food that he had suffered for a week in Zaul.

"I'd die for a pepperoni pizza," he muttered as he followed the others down the corridor.

They entered a small room with bright yellow painted walls and no furniture. On the far side, facing the entrance, were several open hatches with a variety of electrical panels above.

Targon sniffed the air. His face crumpled. "I thought we were getting food?"

"You *will* receive nourishment," said Keela, ushering them to the first hatch. "I will order it for you."

"Okay, but where are the tables to eat at?" Targon pressed.

Keela seemed confused by his comment. "Why would you need tables?" She looked at him for a minute and then turned to press a raised square on the first panel. A small clear cup appeared in the open space at the bottom of the hatch.

"What is your body weight, sir?" she asked Varl.

"One hundred and ninety-seven pounds," he replied. "And my name is Varl."

As if by magic, a thick pink liquid appeared in the cup. Keela looked satisfied and handed it to Varl.

"The computer has taken your body weight into account when preparing this nourishment. This drink contains everything you will need for a healthy existence in the way of proteins, carbohydrates and fats. I am sure that you will find it refreshing."

Varl stared at the cup in horror. He looked at Keela, who smiled sweetly and waited for him to drink.

"I'll wait for the others, if you don't mind," he said quickly. "Where I come from it is tradition not to eat before everyone is served."

Matt could hardly refrain from laughing at Varl's hesitancy to drink. The pink liquid could not possibly taste worse than the slimy green lingoones he'd been given to eat in Zaul. He wondered what Varl would do with a pepperoni pizza.

Keela nodded and turned to Targon. "Body weight?"

Targon looked blankly at her. "I have no idea," he said, turning as pink as the liquid with embarrassment.

Matt looked at Targon's thin frame. "I would guess he's at least twenty pounds lighter than me; around ninety-six."

"No need to guess. Stand on this pad, please," she said, directing Targon to a bright red square, set into the floor in the corner of the room.

A tiny light flickered above the first hatch and the number 98 blinked in neon green on a small screen.

"I was close," mumbled Matt. "Pretty good estimate, if you ask me."

Targon's complexion turned quickly white as the pink liquid appeared in a cup and the article was placed carefully in his hands.

"One hundred sixteen," said Matt, before she could ask.

"Thank you." Keela punched in the numbers on a small

vertical keyboard. The computer registered 116, and another cup was filled. "Drink up, there is more to follow."

Targon retched. "More of this?"

Keela laughed. "Oh, no! Something that tastes even better."

Targon grimaced. He whispered to Matt. "What else do you think she has in store for us?"

Varl took the plunge and tasted the drink. He smiled. "It's okay, boys. Quite nice really. Tastes like some kind of sweet fruit."

"Strawberry, I think," said Matt, taking a sip and licking his lips.

"What's strawberry?" asked Targon.

"A bright red juicy fruit that I often eat back home. It's good, honestly."

Targon raised the cup slowly to his lips and stuck his tongue into the liquid. He looked relieved by its taste and quickly drank the rest.

Keela had moved on to the second hatch and again entered their body weights into the computer. She handed each of them a small plate on which there were two tablets in different shades of blue.

"The rest of your nutrition requirement," she said proudly. "The first tablet contains all the vitamins your body needs daily, and the second contains minerals, iron, calcium and other necessities for healthy growth."

"This is *it*?" said Targon, scowling.

"Until tomorrow at this time," said Keela. She closed the hatches.

"Tomorrow?" repeated Matt, practically choking on the

last salty tablet. In Zaul he had been reduced to two meals a day and now in Karn, only one. At this rate he'd be as thin as Targon within a week!

"What more would you require?" asked Keela. "Your body is being well looked after."

"But my stomach feels empty. It's rumbling with hunger," Targon complained.

"I am sorry, but I do not understand the rumbling that you are describing. I will ask Sorrol what that means."

Varl collected the cups and placed them on the hatch. "Thank you, Keela," he said gently, "I'm sure we'll be just fine."

Matt and Targon looked at him with surprise. Surely Varl hadn't been satisfied by that meal?

Keela walked to the door. "And now if you would accompany me to the meeting room, the Elders wish to interrogate you."

Targon's face changed when he heard the word interrogate. Matt could see the uncertainty reappear in his friend's eyes. Varl was harder to read, although he looked uncomfortable. Matt felt surprisingly calm. Instinct told him that if he were in any danger he would not have been fed first. *Nourishment—not food*, he thought, *there's a big difference.*

Keela led the way down yet another gleaming metallic tunnel. Matt noted the markings on the sides. The writing in Area 4 was in blue, not red. Apart from that, there was little to distinguish their route from any of the other corridors he had been down since arriving in Karn.

They reached a wide door, which was split horizontally

across the middle. The two halves slowly separated. As the bottom half disappeared into the floor, Keela stepped over the metal groove and led them into the meeting room.

Matt smiled as he studied the furnishings. A dozen rows of plush, cushioned chairs stood in a semicircle facing a long stone table. Brass lamps, shining against pale yellow walls, created a warm, welcoming atmosphere.

"If you would like to take a seat, the Elders will join you shortly," said Keela, showing them to the middle three chairs in the front row.

"I'll sit between you, if you don't mind. I'd feel safer," whispered Targon after Keela had left. "What do you think they'll do to us?"

"Not sure," Varl replied. "I don't get the feeling that we're in any imminent danger. However, until we know exactly where we are, and what these people are like, I'll reserve judgment."

Matt leaned across Targon to talk to Varl. "By my reckoning, they wouldn't have fed us if they're about to throw us to the wolves."

"Throw us to the wolves?" said Targon, horrified.

"Relax, it's only a 2010 expression," replied Matt.

"You could be right," agreed Varl. "Let's hope these people are willing to communicate and see reason."

"Are they people?" said Matt. "I mean, are they actually human?"

Varl stared at Matt. "What would make you think otherwise? They speak English, eat, breathe, wear clothing . . . they're not androids."

"But they speak in a stilted way—almost like a computer-generated voice. Every word is pronounced so clearly and precisely. It's eerie! *And* their skin has a golden glow. I've never seen anything like it before. What about those weird markings on their necks—surely you've both noticed the parallel lines?"

Varl nodded in agreement. "True, they could be androids built to look like humans, and I can't deny the thought hadn't occurred to me. Although, if that's the case, these are near-perfect examples."

"You're not saying that you think they're Cybergons in another form, are you?" Targon cut in, fidgeting nervously in his seat.

Varl continued. "As I always say, anything is possible where technology is concerned. I am sure that not all androids are necessarily a threat to humanity."

Targon was on the edge of his chair. "With only one exception, every android *I've* ever known has been!"

A small door on Matt's left began to open. The halves moved apart, quickly disappearing into the floor and the ceiling. Two middle-aged figures swept into the room. One appeared to be male; the other, female. They wore identical tight black pants and long-sleeved tops. Brightly colored tunics covered their garments, tied at the sides in several places and reaching almost to their ankles. The couple sat down at the table facing Matt, Targon, and Varl.

The tall female, with neatly cropped gray hair and fine features, folded her hands carefully on her lap. She was the first to speak. "Welcome to the Realm of Karn. My name is Marcella, and this is Calute. We are two of the ten Elders who rule the people of Karn. This initial evaluation is necessary so that we can establish who you are and what you are doing in our realm."

Varl immediately counteracted with his own questioning. "Should we be afraid that we're here in Karn?" he asked bravely.

"Not unless you prove to be any threat to our existence," Calute quickly answered. He pushed his black rimmed glasses up the bridge of his nose. "We are a peaceful people already struggling for survival, and we will not tolerate any further threat to our community."

"That is understood," replied Varl. "We're not here to harm you in any way, and we wish to leave as quickly as possible. My name is Varl. These boys are Targon and Matt. Targon and I are from the Kingdom of Zaul and Matt is from . . ."

"The United States," Matt cut in, realizing that he had never told Varl where he was from—just the time period.

"We have not heard of either of these places. How do you come to be in Karn?" Marcella asked.

"We're not really sure . . ." began Varl.

Matt had never seen him at a loss for words, but on this occasion Varl seemed to be having trouble knowing where to begin.

"Could you please tell us what year this is?" asked Matt, helping Varl out. Matt prayed that the advanced technology of Karn might help him understand their situation.

"This is Earth in the year 2540 AD," replied Marcella.

Varl gasped. "Really?" He looked at Targon and then at Matt.

"You seem alarmed," said Marcella. "Are you time

travelers?"

Varl chuckled. "I'm afraid our situation is very complex. Targon and I are also from the year 2540, and yet we haven't heard of Karn, and you haven't heard of Zaul."

"That does not surprise me," Calute said, twiddling the ends of his long pointed mustache. "As I am sure that you are aware, Earth in 2540 consists of thousands of small kingdoms. Many are primitive, many advanced in their technology, and many are at war. Each of us is only familiar with those kingdoms in close proximity to our own."

Varl nodded. "I've no doubt that you're correct. Our situation is somewhat confused by Matt here, who claims that he is . . ."

" . . . from Earth in the year 2010," Matt cut in quickly, deciding that any mention of them all being characters in his computer game was not wise. Calute and Marcella would just laugh at him. Matt suspected that even Varl was still not convinced by his arguments. What hope would he have convincing the Karns without having his computer as proof? He stared at Varl and Targon hoping that they understood why he didn't say anything more.

Matt took a deep breath before attempting some kind of explanation. "Yes, Marcella, we *are* time travelers. I landed in Zaul by accident. When I tried to leave Zaul and get back to my own time, I found myself here in Karn. I seem to have mistakenly brought along my friends from Zaul."

"You do not *seem* to be a very good time traveler!" said Calute, sounding somewhat skeptical. He stared at Matt over the top of his spectacles.

"I guess not. We're still experimenting with time travel in

2010," lied Matt. He looked into Calute's piercing ebony eyes.

"We have met others like you," said Marcella, "but never from as far back as 2010. The Karns believe that time travel won't be fully developed until two hundred years from now—sometime in the 2700's."

"So you've no way of transporting us out of here?" asked Varl.

Calute played with his mustache again. "I am sorry. Those who have landed here before you came from *our* future, and have returned to their own times using their own equipment and transportation devices. Matt, have you *no* method by which you can return home?"

"Possibly. I've a small personal computer—but it seems to have disappeared on our journey. If I can find it, we may be able to leave Karn."

"A lot of things *seem* to have happened," muttered Calute in a hostile tone.

"Describe this computer to me," said Marcella. She rolled up her sleeves and placed her hands firmly on the table.

"Where I come from it is called a laptop—a small black box about an inch deep." Matt demonstrated by spreading his thumb and forefinger apart. "I don't suppose you've found anything like that?"

"I am sorry to disappoint you, but nothing like you describe has been handed to us. We will send notification to all Areas. Perhaps it will appear soon." Marcella whispered to Calute and then looked back at Matt. "There is one other possibility, but you will not like to hear of it."

"And that is?" asked Varl, frowning.

"It is possible that the boy's computer landed somewhere in Areas 6 to 12." Marcella took a deep breath and paused. "If that is the case, it will not be easy to retrieve."

"And why is that?" Varl asked.

"Evil Noxerans have taken over the Realm of Karn. We Karns live in fear under their enforced laws. We are confined in Areas 1 to 5 and only allowed in Areas 6 to 12 under certain conditions. If you are caught in Areas 6 to 12 without permission you will be imprisoned and possibly executed by the Noxerans."

Targon gulped. "Are they androids?"

Marcella seemed surprised by his question. "The Noxerans—androids? Certainly not! They are *very* human. Humans possess evil qualities that you would never see in an android."

Targon swallowed hard and said nothing further, but Matt guessed he was thinking about the Cybergons back in Zaul, evil beyond belief.

Matt bit his lip. He looked at the three parallel lines on each side of Marcella's neck and her golden complexion. Calute also displayed the same characteristics. Were they androids, humans or something else?

"I guess we are lucky that we landed where we did," said Varl, breaking the awkward silence.

"You have no idea *how* lucky," said Calute ominously.

Chapter 3

Varl stepped out of the pod and followed Keela down yet another tunnel-like corridor. He shielded his eyes from the piercing lights that reflected off the curved metallic walls. After the darkness of the pod, it took him a while to adjust. Keela didn't seem to experience any difficulty adapting to the light—she jogged clumsily along in front, her large feet appearing awkward under her slender frame. Matt and Targon ambled behind, discussing the experience of being below sea level. Neither boy seemed to find the bright lighting a problem. Varl decided that he was getting old, and that his eyes were failing. He rubbed them gently and squinted to see where he was walking.

Varl had never seen the ocean before, but he had often read about the wonders that lay beneath the surface in many of the old textbooks that he had preserved. He was mesmerized by the variety of sharks and the broad assortment of reef fish that swam close to the pod's transparent tunnel. He walked in silence, reflecting on the beauty he had just witnessed.

They turned the corner. A large courtyard, decorated with lush tropical plants in elegant brass planters, confronted Varl. He stood with his mouth wide open. The hexagonal room was constructed of a reinforced transparent material within a lattice framework. Through it he could watch more of the breathtaking beauty surrounding Karn. The lights were dim within the enclosure, but outside, the reef seemed magically illuminated.

Varl looked up to witness a school of iridescent orange fish dart across the roof. He sank into one of the comfortable couches and sat, hypnotized by the colorful creatures that swam beyond the glass divider.

"Welcome to Area 3," announced Keela with pride. She took hold of her sleek black hair and tossed it behind her shoulders. "Area 3 consists of sleeping quarters and every leisure facility necessary for a balanced daily life. We have areas for relaxation and areas for fitness maintenance. This is one of our many mind-relaxing courtyards. I am sure that during your stay with us in Karn, you will find it soothing and restful to sit and watch the marine life."

"It's truly beautiful," said Varl, still captivated by the color and enormous variety of sea creatures. Even Targon and Matt stood in silent awe.

"It is time for you to see your quarters. You will be able to return here later," said Keela, heading for the exit.

Varl sighed and reluctantly dragged himself off the comfortable sofa.

"Shame," he grumbled. "I could sit here all day."

A low rumbling suddenly shook the area. Varl grabbed the fabric arm of the couch to steady himself. Targon and Matt staggered about in an effort to maintain their balance. The tropical plants, in their elaborate pots, jiggled a few inches across the floor, and the lights momentarily flickered. Even the thick transparent windows seemed to vibrate dangerously in their frames. Varl half expected the panels to give way and the water to come cascading in on them. He looked across the room at Keela, who clutched the door frame.

"What's happening?" he hollered.

"Nothing to be concerned about," she shouted above the noise and vibrations. "We get this from time to time. There is a fault line near us, that is all. This is a minor tremor. It will soon pass."

But her expression told Varl otherwise. He studied the girl's exquisite dark features. He could read beyond the tough exterior that she was displaying for their benefit. Varl could see real fear in the deep brown centers of her eyes. Keela was terrified. She clenched the door frame so tightly that her knuckles turned white. Targon fell to his knees, apparently unable to stay upright.

The rumbling finally ceased. It had lasted only seconds, but it had seemed like minutes. Matt pulled Targon to his feet, and together they pushed the plants back into their position by the entrance. Keela calmly straightened her clothing and smiled as if it were all part of daily life in Karn.

"Must be what an earthquake feels like," said Matt. "I've always wondered."

"What's an earthquake?" asked Targon.

"Zaul doesn't lie near a fault line," explained Varl, "so you would never have felt anything like that before. Two plates, which lie close together and form part of the Earth's crust, shift their position. Above ground, when this happens, buildings fall and kingdoms can be destroyed within seconds. The seabed is no different. The sudden movement of the Earth causes a shock wave in the water that becomes a tidal wave on the surface."

Targon shuddered. "Then Karn could be destroyed if the earthquake were big enough?"

Before Varl had a chance to answer, Keela cut in and abruptly changed the subject. "It is getting late. I must show you to your living suite. Please follow me."

Targon looked at Varl and shrugged. Varl winked back. Keela was obviously upset by the talk of the destruction of Karn—perhaps rightly so. He would have plenty of time to explain the Earth's geology, and the Richter scale by which earthquakes were measured, to Targon later.

Keela showed them to a suite of rooms located within yards of the courtyard, and dug into one of her pockets.

"You will need an identification chip," she said, handing them each a small translucent disc attached to a leather cord. "The discs have been programmed to register who you are and allow you access to your room. Make sure that you place the disc firmly against the wall pad." Keela demonstrated.

Varl stared in disbelief as the doors moved apart, and he could see the comfortable accommodation within. The furnishings were soft, and the decorating style, colorful and homey. He entered slowly and touched one of the small lamps, which were arranged in pairs around the windowless room. They cast elongated shadows over the pale yellow walls.

Matt and Targon followed him into the room.

"Isn't this great compared to furniture in Zaul?" Matt asked, turning circles in the center of the room. "I guess this must seem like paradise to you guys," he muttered.

Varl ran his hands across the soft cushions and velvet fabric of the elegant sofa while Targon examined the large video screen built into the far wall.

Keela hovered in the doorway. "The identification chips will also allow you access to any of the common rooms within Area 3. You may visit the fitness room, relaxation room, entertainment center, or health spa. You will see by the number on the door that you have been allocated Living Suite 374. If there is nothing else that I can do for you, I shall leave you now."

"No, this is just perfect," said Varl, with a huge grin. Embarrassed that he was acting like a child instead of an adult, he tried to conceal his excitement and added, "I am sure that we will be very comfortable here. Thank you."

"I hope that you will all feel refreshed after a good night's sleep. There are plenty of clean clothes in the closets and a herbal spa in the bathroom. You will be awakened by the daily fitness program on the room monitors."

"Herbal spa?" said Targon.

"Awakened by a fitness program?" repeated Matt with a disapproving expression.

"You will see in the morning. I will come for you shortly after the program concludes," Keela continued. "Calute and Marcella wish to see you again after they have reported to the Meeting of Elders."

"And what exactly is the Meeting of Elders?" asked Varl.

"Whenever there is a problem in Karn, the Elders meet to decide what to do."

"A government, in other words," concluded Varl.

"Correct. Now, if there is nothing else, I must say

goodnight." Keela bowed her head and gave a small curtsy before backing through the door.

Two bedrooms adjoined a central lounge, each with its own private bathroom. Varl checked out his accommodation and then sauntered into the bedroom that Matt was to share with Targon.

He stood in the doorway, scratching his rough chin. "No shaving equipment in my bathroom," he announced. "I'll have to go another day with this stubble."

Varl glanced around the bedroom. The bunk beds were molded into the wall. Each had a springy mattress and a small rectangular silver blanket folded at one end. Matt was already examining the fabric.

"Hope this is thick enough to keep me warm," he said, fingering the flimsy material.

"It looks good enough to me," said Targon. He repeatedly pressed his hand down on the mattress with a delighted grin on his face.

Matt opened the closets and pulled out several tunic tops in a variety of bright colors and styles. In the drawer beneath, numerous pairs of black pants and zippered tops were folded neatly. He stuck out his tongue and held them up for Varl to see.

"Don't worry, they'll look great on you," teased Varl. "The blue tunic is just your color, and I'm sure Targon will look good in green!"

"I think I like Zaul fashion better. Your baggy pants and T-shirts are definitely preferable," Matt moaned. "Can't say I've ever seen myself in a tunic."

"Well, this is just great," said Targon happily. He hauled

himself on to the upper bunk. "I think I'm going to like it here."

"Zang it, Targon! Let's get this in perspective," said Matt, raising his voice. He sat on the lower bunk with a long face. "This may all be very nice, but it sure isn't home for any of us!"

"Very nice?" shot back Targon, leaning over the edge and peering down at him. "That's an understatement! What are the words you taught me from 2010? 'Too cool'? Yes, that's it. This place is better than anything I've *ever* seen—except for the food, of course."

"*Nourishment*, not food," corrected Matt. "There's a definite difference. All this talk about fitness maintenance—I don't think any of us will survive on such a disgusting diet for long, even if it is a healthy alternative. My stomach's been rumbling for hours. Besides, Targon, I thought you longed for sunshine and the beautiful mountains of Zaul after being held prisoner by the Cybergons for so long. I can guarantee you won't feel any sun on your face three hundred feet below sea level!"

Targon shrugged. "I've lived without sunshine long enough, and at least I'm not a slave here. Besides, this place has a beauty all of its own."

"Indeed it does," agreed Varl, who until now had refrained from entering the discussion. He left the doorway and walked across the room. Thoughtfully, he sat down next to Matt and sighed as he felt the thick mattress give slightly below the weight of his body. "Much as I hate to admit it, Matt is right. It is easy to forget why we are here when the surroundings are so comfortable and the people so pleasant."

"And why *are* we here?" grumbled Targon. "Nobody knows! Matt can't even answer that. Perhaps we were meant to be here—and I'm certainly not in any hurry to return to Zaul. I can't wait to check out the entertainment room!"

"Well, I'm sorry that you feel like that," said Matt, "although I understand why. I wouldn't be keen to return to Zaul either. But I *am* in a hurry to get back to *my* home, which suddenly seems wonderful. I'm really beginning to miss it. Don't think I'll complain about broccoli ever again!"

"What's broccoli?" asked Targon, swinging his legs close to Matt's head.

"A green vegetable. You'd like it," replied Matt. He looked up at Targon. "I haven't forgotten how you stuffed lingoones down your throat in Zaul. If you like lingoones, you'd like broccoli. Anyway, I need to find my computer. I have this horrible feeling that . . ."

"You're still playing your *Keeper of the Kingdom* game," Varl finished Matt's sentence, chuckling to himself. "I thought you'd say that." He had been wondering when Matt would bring up the subject of his computer game.

Matt chewed his bottom lip. "If that's the case, I need to get instructions to continue playing or I might never get home."

"Well, I vote that Matt finds his computer, and Varl and I stay and enjoy the Realm of Karn," said Targon defiantly.

"Aren't you the least bit curious as to how you got here?" asked Varl.

"No," said Targon without a moment's thought.

Varl sighed. "Well, I am. I need to know whether this *is* time travel that I've had the pleasure of experiencing, or whether we really are in some computer game, as Matt here would have us believe. I won't be happy until I know for sure. I guess it's the scientist in me—always searching for answers."

"Thanks, Varl," said Matt. "If we can find my computer, I might be able to give you those answers."

"And I suppose you'll want my help?" said Targon in an annoyed tone.

"Well, it would be nice," replied Matt. "Besides, I don't think you'd survive long on mental relaxation techniques and vitamin pills!"

And even if Targon can, I won't, thought Varl.

* * * * *

Marcella stood in the corner watching Calute walk back and forth in front of the door of the Elders' chamber. The room was small but comfortable, and totally soundproof. Ten high-backed chairs were positioned around a central rectangular table supported by two granite pedestals. The solid interlocking doors in Area 1 were designed for protection against flooding. In an emergency, the entire population of Karn could take refuge within its walls.

Calute smoothed his black hair over his ears, and chewed on his bottom lip. She guessed he hadn't slept well. The strangers had caused her a sleepless night also.

"I am not happy with our situation," said Calute angrily. "We have no real knowledge of where these strangers are from, or why they are here, and you are willing to believe their story without any real evidence that what they say is true.   Have you ever heard of time travelers losing the method by which they travel?" He looked at her over the top of his glasses. "It sounds phony."

"And what else would you have us do?" asked Marcella. "If the boy *did* have a computer that they used for time travel, then it is in our best interests to help them find it and to get them all out of here quickly!"

Calute reached the far wall. He pivoted on his heels and turned back toward Marcella.

"And, by allowing them the freedom to wander around at their leisure, what if they pose a threat to our plans? What then?   The Freedom Fighters have worked for months preparing for our rebellion against the Noxerans. We cannot let anything get in the way now."

Marcella was outraged. "What are you suggesting—that we lock up two boys and an old man in the prison until it is all over?" she shouted. "That could be weeks, Calute! Even you could not be that heartless."

Calute sat down in one of the high-backed chairs. He folded his hands behind his head and sighed wearily. "Then I do not know what we should do, Marcella. How do we know that they are not spies sent by the Noxerans? Besides, the longer the strangers are here, the more they will learn about our situation."

Marcella walked to stand in front of him. "Call it instinct," she said softly. "I *believe* they are time travelers who have had the misfortune to land in Karn at an inappropriate moment. Who would send two boys and an old man on a spying mission?"

"The Noxerans," snapped Calute. "They are devious and

cunning—but you already know that. Besides, you have to admit, the old man, Varl, looks like one of the Noxeran Senate members."

"But I am not often wrong, am I?" retorted Marcella.

"This time, you cannot afford to be," said Calute, playing with the ends of his dark mustache. "I suggest that we put the old man and the boys to a test."

Marcella was intrigued. She sat down in the chair next to him and said, "What have you in mind?"

"We send them into Area 6 to locate the boy's computer."

"That could be a death sentence!" Marcella was horrified. "You cannot be serious. If these *are* genuine time travelers, could you live with yourself if they die at the hands of the Noxerans?"

"And can you live with yourself if we jeopardize the rebellion—and the lives of everyone in Karn—because you took pity on strangers?"

Marcella slumped in her chair. "I wish there were another way."

"Okay, perhaps that idea is a little harsh. What if we explain the situation to the old man without revealing anything more than he needs to know? Then we will see how keen they are to retrieve the boy's computer, knowing that the odds are against them."

"I do not like playing games, Calute."

"If they back away from finding the computer when we tell them about Area 6, we will know the computer is not important to them, and they are not time travelers. If, on the other hand, they devise a plan that shows they have inside knowledge of the Noxeran organization, we will also know to treat them with caution."

"And what if it becomes obvious that these strangers have no knowledge of the Noxerans and insist on walking blindly into Area 6?"

"Then we will help them as much as we can. Will you support this idea if I suggest it to the Meeting of Elders?" asked Calute, getting to his feet.

Marcella nodded reluctantly. "All right," she muttered. "I am not happy, but I see no other alternative."

"It is agreed, then. Thank you, Marcella, for your cooperation."

A loud clunk preceded the opening of the heavy interlocking door. The two halves slid apart, and a breathless young man with straggly shoulder-length hair barged into the room.

"Marcella, Calute, I am instructed to inform you that the Meeting of Elders has to be postponed," he gasped.

"Postponed? Why?" demanded Calute.

"A matter of utmost urgency has arisen!"

"And what, Sorrol, could be more urgent than the arrival of three strangers in Karn?" Calute yelled at the young man.

"Braymar has been captured by the Noxerans, sir!"

"Braymar? Surely not!" Marcella sank into her chair, hardly believing what she had heard. "Now our rebellion will fail. Without the leader of the Freedom Fighters, what chance do we have for success?"

"Little, I fear," said Calute, brows lifting. "Is this certain, Sorrol?"

"Braymar was on a scouting mission in Area 6. We have reports that he was caught tampering with Noxeran machinery and is now being held prisoner in Area 8. Some of the Elders fear that he will be killed before we can negotiate with the Noxeran Senate for his release."

"Are the reports confirmed?"

"Not as yet, sir. The Elders will meet with you late tomorrow when more is known about Braymar's position. You are instructed to take care of the three strangers in whatever manner you choose."

"Thank you, Sorrol," said Marcella softly.

The sections of door slid closed, like two pieces of a jigsaw puzzle that fit perfectly together.

"And now what?" Marcella asked Calute.

"Nothing changes. We continue as planned."

Chapter 4

Matt fidgeted in his chair. The glittery blue tunic chafed around his neck, and the black pants were too tight around his thighs—he'd rather wear his baggy jeans any day. But at least the clothes were clean. He looked across at Targon, who chewed anxiously on his fingernails, and then at Varl, who stared intently at the table in front. Neither seemed bothered by their new attire.

Marcella and Calute were late, and the waiting was not easy. Each passing minute made Matt feel more afraid. What had the Elders decided? Had they believed his story?

The small door divided, and Marcella entered the meeting room bearing a grim expression. Her perfect golden skin was furrowed across her brow. Calute followed closely behind. He seemed tense and irritated as he placed a small box, no bigger than a paperback book, down on the granite table.

"Thank you for your patience," he began. "Unfortunately, we were detained by other urgent matters."

Targon clutched his seat, and Varl cleared his throat. Matt felt slightly more optimistic. After all, until now they had been treated in a fair and humane manner. He smiled at Marcella, hoping that she might reassure him by her expression, but she remained poker-faced.

Calute walked around to the front of the table and stood

before them. "After careful consideration, the Elders have decided to support your efforts to locate your computer."

"Thank you," said Varl, relaxing. A smile crept across his face.

Matt sighed with relief and then caught his breath. Marcella didn't look pleased. Perhaps all the news was not so good.

Calute stroked his chin with the tip of his forefinger. "We have made a thorough search, and there have been no reports of a personal computer such as you have described anywhere in this half of Karn."

"Great," whispered Targon. "I'm not eager to go back to Zaul anyway."

Varl jabbed him in the ribs angrily and directed another question at Calute. "What do you suggest we should do? Without Matt's computer we have no way to leave Karn."

"We believe that your computer may be somewhere in Areas 6 to 12. Most probably in Area 6."

Matt smiled. At last there was some hope of finding his laptop and trying to discover what went wrong. "Well, that's good, isn't it? We can get permission to search these areas, can't we?" he asked eagerly.

Calute played with the ends of his mustache thoughtfully before responding. "You may remember we told you yesterday that those areas are under the control of the Noxerans. We are not allowed to enter any of them without authorization. If your computer has already been discovered, the Noxerans would most likely place something of value in the vault in Area 6. This is the most secure area, and of course, the hardest to get to."

"But surely, if I explain to the Noxerans that we are time travelers looking for our computer, they would give us permission to look for it," said Matt.

Calute shook his head adamantly. "I am afraid not. Most of the areas under Noxeran control are highly restricted. They would not consider allowing you to enter classified areas under *any* circumstances."

Matt jumped to his feet and looked pleadingly into Calute's dark eyes. "But I *have* to find my computer, don't you understand? I can't stay here. I have to get home—we all do!"

Calute gave Marcella a sideways glance. "Then your only other choice is to find a way to enter the Noxeran half of Karn without being seen. It would be far easier for one person to slip in and out than for three of you to attempt to go."

"And how would I do that?" Matt asked without hesitation.

Marcella finally spoke. "It will not be easy. We will let you have the plans of Karn showing you where Areas 6 to 12 are located and how you can move between each."

"And what if the boy is discovered?" snapped Varl.

"Then he will be in serious trouble. The Noxerans do not tolerate intruders and have no compassion for those caught breaking the rules. He will be imprisoned or executed."

Matt gulped. "Without my computer, I might as well be dead. I thank you for your hospitality—and it's not that I don't like Karn—but I have to get home. I *want* to go home. I'll just have to risk getting caught. The Noxerans can't be that bad. Besides, you said they're humans, not androids, so at least I can reason with them."

Calute and Marcella exchanged glances again. Calute raised his eyebrows and Marcella shrugged her shoulders.

"Will you excuse us for a minute?" Calute asked.

He and Marcella walked over to the door and conferred in hushed tones. Matt watched apprehensively, wondering what was being said. After several minutes they returned and stood side by side in front of him.

"All right, we will help you formulate a plan," said Marcella, her expression softening.

"Thank you," said Varl.

Marcella placed her hands gently on Matt's shoulders. "You must understand from the beginning that Calute and I can in no way accompany you on this mission. Our duty as Elders of Karn is to serve *our* people. If we put our own lives in jeopardy, we will not be doing that."

Matt nodded. "Thanks. I know we've asked a lot."

"Without your help, I fear Matt would fail," added Varl.

"And he *still* might," Calute added quickly. He leaned toward Matt and stared into his deep blue eyes. "Make sure that you understand the seriousness of what you are about to undertake. This is no child's adventure game. The Noxerans are ruthless killers. They will not care *why* you are snooping in their corridors—only that you are!"

Matt nodded. *No child's adventure game*? *If only you knew, Calute—this is exactly what it is!* "Thank you for your warning and your concern, Calute. I *do* understand what you are saying, but I don't have any option—other than to stay here in Karn. I *have* to find my computer."

"So be it. Since you are still determined to find a way into Area 6, come up to the table, and I will show you how to operate our techbox. It is not linked to our computer network, but relevant information about Karn has been downloaded onto its memory. You may take it back to your suite and study the plans."

"Thanks," said Matt, approaching the long table. "I really appreciate your help."

"Save your thanks until after your safe return," Calute replied tersely.

He opened the small cream-colored box and demonstrated the necessary functions to Matt. The keyboard was close to the version Matt was familiar with, using the English language, with the letters arranged in the same position. But Matt felt depressed as he handled Karn technology. It became abundantly clear that he would have to find his own computer. Even if he could find his *Keeper of the Kingdom* CD-ROM, the techbox had no CD-ROM drive and would probably be useless. But at least this little computer was something vaguely familiar. It held hope for them all.

The two halves of the door moved apart, and the young Karn, who had escorted Matt, Varl, and Targon from Area 5, strode into the room. He bowed his head slightly at the Elders and approached the table.

"This is Sorrol," announced Marcella. "I believe that you have already met."

Matt stepped back, feeling uneasy in the presence of his captor. He stared at the familiar shiny silver buckle sporting the elaborate 'S'. "Sorrol," Matt mumbled to himself, pleased at least to know his name.

Sorrol maintained his serious expression but began an

apology in his deep voice. "I am most regretful that I was so abrupt with you all. You must understand that any intruder in Karn must be debriefed before pleasantries are exchanged. It is my job to ensure that there is no security threat, and therefore, I treat every individual in the same manner."

Matt smiled at Sorrol's use of language. Even under friendly circumstances, Sorrol seemed so formal and unapproachable. Did this Karn ever relax?

Varl extended his hand and thanked Sorrol for the official welcome.

Targon remained aloof. He stared at the wild-looking young man with the enormous muscles and whispered to Matt. "I don't care how friendly he is, I still don't like the look of him."

"Sorrol and Keela will answer any questions you may have after studying the information on the techbox," said Marcella. "I suggest that you take a day to decide how you are going to continue—if at all."

Calute approached Varl and spoke in hushed tones. "Be sure that you understand the seriousness of what you are planning to attempt. In our opinion, you will be sending the boy to a certain death. It is unfortunate that Marcella and I will be unable to help you today. Other urgent matters have arisen that need our attention. However, we would like to be informed of any plan you put together in case we can be of assistance."

Varl nodded. "Thank you for your help and advice, Calute. We'll look at the plans and let you know what we decide."

* * * * *

Keela giggled. Matt's stomach rumbled and gurgled as he placed the techbox on the table in the center of their suite.

"I will ask Sorrol what we can do to stop this noise your stomach makes," she said, giggling again.

"Good," replied Targon, pulling up the tunic top and patting his bare flesh, "because you might find we die of starvation before too long."

"Die?" said Keela, aghast. Her eyes widened. "You could die from this noise?"

"It's possible," Varl said. He sat down next to Matt and looked up at Keela with a broad grin. "But don't worry, Targon is being a little melodramatic. It would take us weeks to waste away. We won't roll over and die tomorrow."

Targon groaned. "Thanks, Varl, I was hoping we might get something decent to eat if there seemed to be some urgency about it!"

"*However*," Varl continued, "it might be advisable to learn how the Karn body systems function in comparison to our own, so that we can understand whether or not the nutrition we are getting will be adequate."

Keela looked bewildered. "So you really think our nourishment may not be enough to keep you alive?"

Varl pursed his lips. "Let's just say that our bodies may need more bulk than yours do." He turned to Matt, who had begun to open the techbox files. "Any luck, Matt, my boy?"

"Think so," Matt muttered, studying the first file. "Here we go—this is a plan of the Realm of Karn."

Varl leaned closer to the screen. "Hmm! Seems to be a

mighty complex arrangement of areas and connecting corridors."

Matt nodded. "But I'm sure that your caves in Zaul are just as confusing to anyone who isn't familiar with them."

"With one major difference," Varl sighed. "Our caves are not surrounded by water."

Keela laughed. "Those are not corridors, they are pod chutes—like the ones you have traveled in today. Let me explain—it is not difficult to understand." She leaned against the edge of the table and reached across Matt to point to the screen. Her long hair fell forward over her shoulder. "The Realm of Karn was built about one hundred and fifty years ago as a marine research station. It was named for the architect who designed this incredible place—Willard Karn. He was also one of the first to live full-time on Karn."

Targon looked confused. "So where did the Karn people come from originally?"

Keela looked flustered by his question. "I will explain about that later," she said, quickly changing the subject. "The safety of those who would live three hundred feet below the sea was a major concern to the designers, so Karn was planned as an underwater city with a dozen independent areas connected together by pod chutes. In case of a disaster, our Elders can easily isolate one area from the rest."

"Clever," said Varl, scratching his rough chin as he listened.

"Karn is built on the seabed in the shape of two pentagons that lie side by side. Each area is built on three levels for living and working, and forms a point on the pentagon. The sides of the pentagon are formed by the pod chutes. Areas 8 to 12, which the Noxerans have now claimed, are an exact mirror image of Areas 1 to 5."

Matt tapped his fingers against the top of the keyboard as he thought about what Keela had said. "Are you saying that if you know your way around this half of Karn, then you could also find your way around the Noxeran half?"

"Correct," replied Keela. "In fact, all ten areas are laid out in *exactly* the same design."

"I thought you said there were a *dozen* independent areas," interrupted Matt. "You've only mentioned ten."

Keela smiled. "I am glad you were listening. The remaining two areas are designed differently. They will be a major problem."

"And what exactly *is* the problem?" asked Varl.

Keela pointed to the plans. "Areas 6 and 7 lie between the two pentagons and are joined together by thick watertight doors. The pod chute from our half to Area 6 is completely sealed off. The Noxerans removed the pod and flooded the chute so that Karns could no longer get to Area 6."

"So what about the pod chute to Area 7?" Matt questioned.

"The pod chute to Area 7 is guarded by the Noxerans. The Noxerans allow the pod's operation only at certain times of the week. Karns may use it only after obtaining a pass from the Noxeran Senate."

"Presumably the Noxerans can enter any area they choose to?" Varl asked, tapping his fingers at the relevant points on the screen.

"Correct again. They have complete freedom to move anywhere in Karn and may come into our half at any time they want to."

"And do they?" asked Varl.

"Rarely. The Noxerans seem too preoccupied with what they call their 'agenda.'"

"Which is?" probed Varl.

Keela made a sorrowful grimace. "We have no idea what the Noxerans are here to do, although some Karns have tried unsuccessfully to find out. The Noxerans *claim* that they are involved in some kind of geo-thermal project."

"Hmm," said Varl.

There was a moment of silence in the room.

Matt pushed back his chair and stretched his legs. "So, Keela, what you are saying is that we would need a pass to get by the guard into Area 7. Then we'd have to find a way to get through the watertight doors into Area 6."

She smiled. "Exactly. The only link between our half of Karn and the Noxerans' half is the pod chute from Area 7. For the last decade we have existed almost as separate cities, except that Karns are totally at the mercy of the Noxerans."

"And how is that?" asked Varl.

"The computerized life support and oxygen scrubbing systems for all areas of Karn are located in Area 7."

"Which means that if the Noxerans didn't maintain the air system or if they choose to destroy it, all Karns would die," Varl concluded.

Keela hung her head. "We all pray that day will never come."

"That's pretty scary!" said Matt.

"I have said enough," said Keela, looking worried. "The

Elders would not approve of me discussing such things. Let us concentrate on finding a way to get you into Area 6."

"It all sounds too difficult," said Targon, yawning. "We should just enjoy Karn and forget about Matt's computer."

Ignoring Targon's comments and staring at the map on the screen, Varl said, "To sum up our problem, we need a pass to get into Area 7, or we have to find a way to get past the guard without one."

Keela nodded. "I think you understand the situation. There is only one way in and one way out."

"Zang it!" said Matt. "I would say that Targon's right—it's impossible."

Targon laughed. "And I thought I was the pessimist! Since when did the impossible ever stop you before, Matt? Why don't you grow some fins and swim to Area 6?"

There was silence momentarily. Matt stared at Varl. His eyes grew wide with excitement.

"That's it! You've done it again, Targon!" said Matt happily.

"What a bright idea!" Varl praised.

Targon looked horror struck. "I *was* joking," he protested. "You didn't think I was serious . . . did you?"

"Can it be done?" said Varl, turning his attention to Keela.

She shrugged her shoulders. "There is only one major air lock in continual use. It is in Area 7—controlled by the Noxerans, of course. It is used regularly by the Noxerans for arrival and departure, research, and food collection."

"So then there is no way of getting to Area 6 by sea?" asked Varl sadly.

Keela's eyes twinkled excitedly. "There *are* emergency

airlocks for evacuation purposes in all areas of Karn, if that is what you mean. They are much smaller and not very well maintained. There should be one in Area 6, so technically it would be possible."

Varl looked at the plans again. "Yes, here it is," he noted.

"Surely it's to our advantage if the Area 6 airlock isn't frequently used," said Matt.

"True, but . . ." Keela hesitated.

"But what?" asked Matt eagerly. "Is the water too deep to dive . . . or too cold?"

"The water *is* warm enough in these parts and we have got old diving gear stored in Area 5, but of course there are other things to worry about."

"Like?" Matt pressed.

"Like sharks—tiger sharks, to be precise."

"Sharks?" Targon cut in. "Whoa! That's it! Now you guys have to be serious. You can't possibly consider this idea."

"And what else, Keela?" asked Matt, still interested.

Targon stared at Matt with an open mouth. "Isn't that enough?"

"And?" Matt pressed again.

"Decompression," replied Keela softly.

"What's that?" asked Targon.

"Decompression sickness is caused by the absorption of nitrogen into the body," Varl explained. "Humans breathe in air that is made up of 20% oxygen and 80% nitrogen. We normally exhale nitrogen through respiration. But when you dive to certain depths, and then swim to the surface too quickly, the body can't get rid of the nitrogen fast enough."

"So, explain please—what would that do to you?" asked Targon, trying to understand Varl's explanation.

"You wouldn't want to know," said Matt glumly.

"You would get what is called 'the bends'," Varl continued. "Nitrogen begins to bubble in the blood and in your joints. If nitrogen bubbles in your spinal column, you could be paralyzed for life. Decompression sickness is at best painful, and at worst, deadly."

Keela ran her fingers through her long hair and wrapped the ends tightly around her fingers. "I am afraid that I have to agree with Targon—swimming to Area 6 is not an option. Karn is pressurized to sea level. If you were swimming to an area where you knew you could get straight into a recompression chamber, you *might* be able to wear the old diving gear and survive. But in three hundred feet of water, to swim around to Area 6 and perform a task in another area also pressurized to sea level, you would get decompression sickness for sure. The Noxerans would happily watch you die."

Targon dragged a chair from the other side of the room and sat down at the table. "It was a dumb idea, anyway," he muttered.

"No, it wasn't," said Varl emphatically. "That's *got* to be our way in, and it's the way the Noxerans would least expect. So, I suggest we stop the pessimism and get to work thinking about how it can be done!"

Chapter 5

"Sorrol, any news?" asked Marcella anxiously, as he stepped through the dividing door of the Elders' Chamber.

Calute got to his feet to hear the report. "Well?" he demanded, before the young man had time to walk toward him.

"Not good. I am sorry. Our intrepid leader of the Freedom Fighters, Braymar, *is* being held hostage in Area 8. Princeps Nonius Balbus, leader of the Noxeran Senate, has demanded an immediate meeting with Karn Elders. You and Calute are instructed to be at the pod chute to Area 7 with the others at nine tomorrow morning. There will be passes waiting for you."

"Thank you, Sorrol," said Marcella sadly. "It is as we feared."

Calute's mouth dropped. "This will be the end of our plans to reclaim Karn. The Noxerans will double security and hold us all accountable. I dread to think what the consequences might be."

"That will be all. Thank you, Sorrol," said Marcella.

"There is one other item that needs your attention, Elder Marcella," added Sorrol. "Keela has brought the three strangers to see you. She is waiting outside and wants to know if you will see them here in the Elders' Chamber, or if she should take them to the meeting room."

"Tell Keela to give us a few minutes, and then she may bring them in."

The door closed behind Sorrol, and Calute banged his fist angrily on the circular table. "Why did Braymar have to be so stubborn? I warned him that Noxeran security had been increased, and it was not a good time to go on another scouting mission—but he insisted."

"He meant well, and he *has* returned safely on many other occasions," replied Marcella.

"Agreed, but this is not one of them!" Calute snapped.

"Passes into the Noxeran half of Karn will now be like gold," Marcella added sadly.

"*And* the Noxerans now realize that we Karns are not sitting idly by and allowing their flagrant abuse of our rights. Now they *know* we are plotting against them. They will watch us closely."

"Be thankful that on this occasion Braymar used his official pass to gain access to Area 6. At least the Noxerans do not know the secret of the Karn people, and we will be able to use it when we carry out our rebellion."

"Pity he did not stay in the areas he was supposed to," said Calute bitterly. "A few more months and we would have succeeded in ridding Karn of the Noxerans. Now it will take longer."

Marcella got to her feet and grasped Calute's hand gently. "At least Braymar can be trusted. He will keep the secret of the Karn people. That is most important for any future attempt to reclaim our realm. Tomorrow, after the meeting with the Noxeran Senate, we will have to reassess the situation."

"You are always a calming influence, Marcella, and right as usual. I must save my energy for devising a scheme to get Braymar out of there."

"Are you ready to see Keela and the strangers?"

Calute lifted his head and pursed his lips, causing his mustache to curl upward. "Okay—let us deal with the next problem. Do we trust them?"

Marcella chuckled. "You already know my thoughts on the matter. I would say that our meeting with the three strangers yesterday supported my point of view. The boy's computer is obviously of extreme importance. They seem genuinely desperate to return home."

"True. And they have shown no aggression toward us."

"You have to admit, Calute, that only those who have not experienced the terror of the Noxerans would be foolhardy enough to attempt such a mission."

"Well, at this point we do not have a lot to lose, since our own plans have now been ruined."

"Shall I let them in?"

Calute took his seat at the end of the table and composed himself. "Why not? It is already a bad day—it cannot get much worse," he muttered through clenched teeth.

* * * * *

Varl watched as Keela excitedly squeezed through the crack in the opening door, beckoning Matt and Targon to follow. Varl waited until the door had fully opened before entering the room.

"Welcome, friends," said Marcella. "Please come in." She gestured for them to sit around the large central table.

Varl struggled to pull out one of the heavy, high-backed chairs. He settled himself into the comfortable seat and folded his hands on the table in front of him.

"So," began Calute, "have you thought carefully about everything I said?"

"Indeed," replied Varl. "We still intend to find Matt's laptop, and we've put together a solid plan."

Calute sighed. "Another stubborn one," he mumbled to Marcella. "A *solid* plan, Varl? I think that under the present circumstances you would be well advised to reconsider. If you attempt any kind of mission into the Noxeran half of our realm, you may never be allowed to return."

"And what are the *present circumstances*, exactly?" asked Varl, wondering what could have changed between yesterday's meeting with Calute and the present.

"One of our most brave and clever leaders has been caught spying in Area 6. We fear for his life. The Noxeran Senate wishes to meet with Karn Elders tomorrow morning."

"Oh, I see," said Varl, raising his voice slightly. "And now you expect us to cancel our plans because one of your colleagues has failed on his mission?"

Marcella quickly interrupted. "Varl, it would be pure folly for any of you to attempt an expedition into the Noxeran section under these conditions. Their guards will be on full alert. Surely you can see the wisdom in putting off your plans for a few days?"

Varl struggled to push back the heavy chair. He stood up and clawed at his unshaven chin. "Madam, I'm grateful that you care about our well-being, but you must understand *our* point of view. We *must* retrieve Matt's computer in order to return to our own time." He banged his fist down on the table. "There is no guarantee that the situation in Karn will change in the next few days and that the Noxerans will decrease security again. Indeed, quite the opposite may happen. After your meeting tomorrow, it might become impossible to consider an attempt for months."

"What are you proposing?" asked Calute, also rising. He walked around the table and looked Varl squarely in the eyes. "You are not suggesting an immediate attempt, are you?"

"Indeed, I am. Why not strike now, when they least expect it? The Noxerans won't anticipate another intruder before your meeting tomorrow."

"You want to try *today*?" Calute shouted in disbelief.

There was silence in the room. Calute looked at Marcella. She raised her eyebrows as if she had no idea what to reply to Varl's suggestion.

"I was actually thinking of tomorrow morning—about the same time that you and Marcella are on your way to meet with the Noxeran Senate," replied Varl.

Calute stared at Varl for a second and then muttered "Hmm," under his breath. He paced back and forth in silence. Varl looked at Matt and Targon for support. They had both remained remarkably quiet throughout the discussion.

"Calute, sir," Matt intervened, "I'm sure that if you were in our situation you'd do exactly the same. We all want to go home—and to get us there, I have to find my laptop. We *will* find it—even without your help."

"But obviously," Varl quickly added, "if we've got your support, we stand a better chance of succeeding."

"They have a great plan," Keela chimed in. "I think it would work."

"*Really!*" said Calute, twirling the ends of his mustache. He glared at Keela. "And is that your sense of logic or your desire for adventure telling you that, young lady?"

"Give them a chance, Elder Calute, I beg you. Please hear what Varl has to say," Keela implored.

"I will listen, Varl," said Calute, still pacing back and forth. "But, be certain of this, I will not allow any foolhardy plan that could further endanger the life of my good friend, Braymar."

An idea suddenly came to Varl. He smiled in the knowledge that Calute would be unable to refuse his offer. "And what if our plan to recover Matt's computer could also include the rescue of Braymar?"

Calute stopped dead in his tracks. He turned abruptly, looked briefly at Marcella and then at Varl. "Okay, I am listening. Make it good," he said, his eyes narrowing.

"Keela tells us that Karns still have an old reconnaissance submersible that is in working order. I believe that you consider it to be a museum piece—too outdated for continued use?"

"I can see that Keela has been divulging too much information," said Calute, scowling at her.

Varl continued, undaunted. "What if, with your help, I could make sure that the submersible is in perfect working order and steer it toward the airlock in Area 6? We will time our arrival to coincide with your meeting with the Noxeran

Senate. That way the guards will more likely be on alert in Area 7 between the connecting pod chute and the Senate chamber. Balbus is bound to demand extra protection with so many Karn Elders close to him."

"An assault by sea . . ." muttered Calute.

"Exactly," said Keela, excitedly. "They will never think of that! Any approaching modern vessel would show on their sonar systems, but the old submersible is too small and almost silent."

Varl sensed that he had Calute interested. "I am told that the submersible was built to enable scientific study of the coral reefs. With that in mind, the engineers designed it to move in patterns like those of a large fish common in these waters. The Noxerans would register the submersible just as that—if it did appear on their tracking systems at all."

Calute played with his mustache once again. There was a sparkle in his eyes, and he suddenly seemed more cheerful. "If I remember correctly, I *was* told that it still works," he offered. "I think it is in storage in Area 1."

"It would not take much to transport it to the vessel launch airlock," Marcella contributed.

Varl noted the expression on her face. She bore an excited grin that stretched from ear to ear. Marcella seemed caught up in his idea, but would Calute agree?

"And what guarantee do we have, Varl, that you could make the necessary checks and any repairs to the submersible systems in time for tomorrow morning?" Calute asked.

Varl scratched his growing beard again. "Honestly? None! I can only promise that I will work through the night if need be. I'm not an engineer, but I am a scientist, and a good one—even if I do say so myself."

Matt interrupted. "Please, Elder Calute," he begged. "Surely it's worth a try, isn't it?"

Calute thought for a moment. "And what about when you reach Area 6? What is your strategy for getting past the Noxeran guards?"

Varl was sure his face had turned a deep shade of red. He felt embarrassed. "I haven't got that far . . . yet," he stammered.

"I have to admit, Varl, I admire your guts!" Calute scoffed. "You must either want to return home desperately, or not care too much for your own life." He raised his voice at Varl. "Your *solid plan* is nothing more than a way in. When you get to Area 6, what are you going to do to avoid detection by the Noxerans, to locate Matt's laptop and to free my friend Braymar? Or, are all of those things just *minor* details?"

"I was hoping that we could work together and devise a good plan between us," Varl shouted back. "With your knowledge of the Noxerans and my ingenuity, a joint effort would suit both of our purposes and just might succeed!"

Marcella rose. "Enough arguing," she said calmly. "You both have very valid points. Varl's plan is not nearly good enough, but the basic idea could work. I also think that a strike at the same time as our meeting with the Senate is a great opportunity."

The room shook, and a low rumble broke into the discussion. Marcella clutched the table for support and looked fearful, first at Calute and then at the walls. The noise and tremors increased. The drinking glasses on the tabletop moved slightly, water slopping over the edges.

"Another earthquake?" asked Varl, grabbing the back of the heavy chair to steady himself. "They seem to be incredibly frequent."

Keela clutched the arms of her chair tightly. Her golden complexion had paled noticeably.

"It will be over in a minute," said Calute with confidence. He pulled on one of the long thin ends of his mustache. "We get at least one a day, but they are rarely strong and last but a few seconds."

"Any idea what causes them?" Varl pressed, as the vibrations subsided.

Calute smiled knowingly. "The Noxerans." He drew in breath.

"The Noxerans?" asked Matt and Varl in unison.

Calute moved back to his chair at the end of the table. "Karn has always used geothermal energy for its power supply. By pumping water into the fault line where the crust of the earth is thinnest, we can capture and use the steam given off. This has always been done at a carefully controlled rate. Fifteen years ago the Noxerans arrived with heavy drilling equipment. As far as we know, they have created a greater power supply."

"What are they using this increase in power for?" Varl questioned, taking his seat.

"There is evidence to suggest that it is being redirected to Noxera, which lies on the coast about fifty miles away."

"What do you think causes the earthquakes?" asked Varl.

Calute shrugged. "I wish we knew. That is what

Braymar was investigating when he was caught. Karn Elders were told that if we obeyed Noxeran rules, asked no questions, and kept to ourselves, they would be finished and gone from here in fifteen years. The fifteen years are almost up."

"And so you accepted the conditions?"

"Naturally. There was little else we could do. We are not an aggressive people, and we had women and children to consider. Things were fine for many years, and apart from losing half of our underwater realm, life continued much as before. It was not until four years ago, when the quakes started, that we began to investigate what the Noxerans were doing."

"Doesn't the frequency of these tremors suggest that the Noxeran methods are dangerous? Surely Karn is at risk from a major earthquake!" Varl regretted his last comment before the words had left his mouth. He looked at Keela, who seemed pale with fear, and realized he was not helping matters.

Calute answered his question. "*Indeed* Karn is at risk! Now you can understand why we live in fear of death. If we do not die directly at the hands of our captors, then we may all die soon from the results of their project. Braymar was part of a much larger plan to rid Karn of the Noxerans. Now we must put our plans on hold and wait again to take action."

"Why don't you all just leave? There are plenty of other kingdoms and realms," Targon innocently suggested.

"This is our home, and it has been the home of the people of Karn for over two centuries. We are used to the underwater life. None of us have any desire to live back on dry land." Marcella explained.

"Besides, why should we be forced to leave our home?" asked Calute indignantly. "All through time, nations have been repressed by tyrants who have conquered their lands and made the people slaves. We are just another such example. It is time for us to rise up and fight for what is rightfully ours!"

Varl offered his hand. "Calute, I can see that you are an intelligent and wise leader. The people of Karn need help as we also need help. I'm begging you to work with me. Together we can free Braymar and rid Karn of the Noxerans."

"Okay," said Calute, in a more controlled tone. "I can see that you mean well." He reached across the table and shook Varl's hand firmly. "I will work with you for the good of Karn and because Marcella believes you to be honest individuals. I hope that I am not making a mistake by placing my trust and Braymar's life in your hands."

"You won't be sorry," replied Varl.

"I hope not. I will find two of our best engineers to help you check the submersible's systems."

Varl smiled. "Rest assured, Calute, that I'll work around the clock to make this expedition a success."

Chapter 6

Matt entered the storage room in Area 1 and walked around the metallic gray frame of the submersible. He'd never seen anything like it. Long and curved at the nose, the vessel resembled a dolphin—even down to the fins on its belly and on the rear of the craft. A small elevator mechanism, which didn't seem capable of such a task, raised the old submersible several feet off the floor. Matt realized that *old* was a relative term. What was old in 2540 AD was still advanced for his world of 2010.

"This is awesome," said Targon, who had never before seen the sea, never mind a submarine. He delighted in using Matt's vocabulary just as Matt had adopted words from Zaul.

Matt grinned. Targon was frightened by his laptop to begin with. *If it's hard for me to come to terms with this kind of technology, then it must be unbelievably difficult for Targon,* he thought.

"How many people can it carry?" Matt asked Keela, who stood proudly in front of the vessel.

"Three, four at a push, I think—but it would be very cramped," she replied.

Matt stared in disbelief. He couldn't imagine two people squeezing into such a confined space—never mind four.

Varl had already crawled into the engine compartment. Two of Karn's finest engineers explained the various systems. Occasionally the word, "unbelievable!" or "incredible!" would be heard above the banging of tools as Varl explored the capabilities of the machine. Finally he emerged, wiping his hands on an old cloth and sweating profusely. It must have been hot in the tiny enclosure.

"Well?" asked Matt, eager to hear his findings.

"This is *almost* technology from my youth!" he replied excitedly. "Before the Cybergons took over Zaul, we humans were using similar power systems."

"Awesome!" said Targon again. "Does that mean you know how to fix her up?"

Varl mopped his brow with the same ragged piece of cloth. "Fix her up?" He shook his head.

Matt's face dropped. "She's not seaworthy then?"

"I didn't say that," said Varl, peeling off the coveralls he'd been lent. "I *won't* be fixing her up because she doesn't need fixing up! Karn engineers have given her a clean bill of health." He smiled at the two greasy individuals still working underneath her frame. "I've never seen anything like it. The power system is in prime condition. The body could do with a bit of work if she were going to be used regularly—but for our purposes, she's in fine working order!"

Keela looked flushed and giggled nervously. "Well, I suppose you will be putting your scheme to the test then. It seemed like a game when we planned this. Now I am *really* worried."

Varl placed his hands gently on her petite shoulders. "Thank you for showing concern for the well-being of three strangers you hardly know," he said softly. "We'll be fine, I promise, and we'll bring back Braymar."

"You . . . you . . . said *we*," stammered Targon. His body

shuddered. "You didn't intend for me to go with you in *that* .
. . *that thing,* did you?" He pointed a finger at the
submersible and twisted his face.

Varl smiled. "Now, Targon, where's that sense of
adventure and incredible bravery that you displayed in Zaul?"
he teased.

"That was different. I knew Zaul—and I couldn't stand
another day living with the Cybergons. I don't fancy getting
the bends you described, and I think I'd die of claustrophobia
if I had to go in that *thing.* I'm quite happy staying here with
Keela in Karn."

"Well, you may be, but I'm not!" retorted Matt. "I'm going
to find my computer—whatever it takes."

"You don't have to come, Targon," said Varl, folding his
coveralls neatly. "Besides, we'll need you here to monitor our
progress."

Targon sighed with relief. "I'm glad we've got that
straight!"

The doors to the storage area opened. Calute entered.
He gingerly approached the submersible and tapped the hull
with his knuckles, creating a dull dead sound. "So, Varl, how
does she look?"

"Not bad at all," Varl responded. "Actually, the
submersible is in very good condition. She's certainly
adequate for our purposes."

"Good. That is good. So, now we are down to those
minor details. What *are* you going to do to avoid detection
when you get there?" Calute asked.

Varl felt the color rising in his cheeks, and his enthusiasm
suddenly dampened. Calute was right. The excitement of

the old submersible and the possibility of finding Matt's computer had carried him away. It was foolish to think that the hard part was getting into Area 6. The hard part was completing their tasks and getting out again.

"I think we had better meet when you are done here," Calute advised.

*   *   *   *   *

Marcella yawned. It had been a long night. She had stayed in the Elders' Chamber making plans with Calute and Varl until the early hours of the morning. Now she regretted it. Both her body and her mind were drained of energy at a time when she needed to be fully alert to meet the Noxeran Senate.

Today she wore her full Karn Elder's regalia—a flowing golden robe with elaborate buttons and a high pointed hat. Her outfit would not be as intimidating to the Noxerans as she would like, but it made her feel better. She was a Karn in a high position, deserving of respect, and she felt proud to represent her people.

There was a loud buzz. Marcella touched the wall pad, and the doors to her suite opened. Calute stood proudly in the corridor. He smiled at her briefly, but she could sense his apprehension.

"Ready?" he asked.

Marcella straightened her hat for the hundredth time and drew in a deep breath. She hesitated on the threshold.

"Hurry up, or we will be late—and that will not put the Noxerans in a good mood for the start of the negotiations,"

Calute nagged. He set off at a fast pace.

Marcella followed hastily. "I am really not looking forward to this," she muttered, catching up with him.

"I am sure that none of us is," Calute replied.

They approached the group of Elders that had gathered by the pod chute and joined the end of the line. The vast assortment of glittering golden robes was reflected in the highly polished walls of the corridor. The Elders stood in silence, waiting for the Noxerans to open the entrance to pod chute 7 and issue them passes to proceed into the Noxeran half of Karn.

Marcella fidgeted with her hat again and shifted her weight nervously from foot to foot. She felt sick. This was not going to be a pleasant experience for any of them. Calute grabbed her hand and squeezed it gently.

"Do not worry, Marcella," he whispered. "Our plan will work, I promise. I have faith in the old man and the boy time traveler. They *will* come back with Braymar, mark my words."

After what seemed like hours of silence, the doors finally parted. A young Noxeran in an ankle-length plain white robe and leather sandals stood sternly on the other side.

"My name is Tacitus," he said in a scratchy voice. "I will accompany you to meet the Noxeran Senate. You will each take a bracelet." He beckoned to another Noxeran who stepped forward from the shadows with an open metal box. "Since the recent invasion of our territory we have changed our pass system."

Horrified by this announcement, Marcella glanced at Calute. Calute's expression in response showed the same shock. They had not anticipated a change in the pass system when formulating plans with Varl.

"Each electronic bracelet is numbered," continued Tacitus, clearing his throat. "It has been keyed into our computer system and pre-programmed. If you stray from the main group and designated areas, or overstay the time allocation, the band will cause you intense discomfort. It will be unlocked and removed from your wrist only on your return." He smiled wryly.

"I can see he takes great pleasure in this," Marcella whispered to Calute. "It is his moment of power."

"Do you have some objection?" Tacitus snapped in a heartless tone. He directed his gaze at Marcella, his eyes narrowing as he waited for her response.

"I just wondered, how much time do we have, exactly?" replied Marcella, thinking quickly. Her stomach churned. She felt like a child who had just been reprimanded, not a respected Karn leader.

"The Senate has allocated four hours for your journey and today's meeting with them. Now, if you will form a single line, a band will be issued to each of you."

"Four hours will be cutting it close," muttered Calute. "I thought Varl and the boy would have longer."

Marcella watched fearfully. One by one the Elders held out their wrists, and the metal bracelet was clipped in place and locked securely. She approached Tacitus and lifted her left hand slowly. Her eyes met his cold, emotionless gaze. He grabbed her wrist roughly and snapped the device in place. It was so tight, Marcella felt as if the blood supply to her fingers would be cut off.

"Next," he shouted.

She hesitated in the doorway. Her mouth was so dry she could hardly speak. "Could you loosen this, please?"

Tacitus gave her a disdainful look. He reinserted the key, made a minor adjustment, and snapped the bracelet closed again. "Now step forward," he sneered.

Marcella did as instructed and followed the others down the winding staircase to pod chute 7. The bracelet was still painful. As she reached the bottom step she tried to adjust it to a more comfortable position on her wrist, but it wouldn't budge. She grimaced as it dug into her flesh. The next four hours would be unbearable.

* * * * *

Matt walked along the metal platform to greet Sorrol. It had taken longer than expected to maneuver the vessel from the storage room into position in the transportation airlock. Attached at the nose by the launch mechanism, and already floating in ten feet of water, the submersible was ready for her first mission in years. Within minutes the huge inlet valves would be opened. Then Sorrol would have to move from where he was standing on the platform and watch the flooding process through the viewing window with Keela and Targon.

The platform shook with every step Matt took. He eyed the fixtures on the wall with suspicion.

"Do not worry," said Sorrol. "The platform is not about to give way. It is designed to flex slightly."

"Thanks," Matt muttered. He felt a little nervous, but the desire to retrieve his laptop and return home was stronger than any fear he had of the Noxerans or the equipment he was about to put to the test.

"Did you enjoy your fish dinner last night?" Sorrol asked.

Matt smiled. "We all did, thank you very much. It was great! Very tasty. I'm sure that we'll do better on this mission with a full stomach."

"Ah! A full stomach and very tasty, you say. That is something we Karns do not understand. But I am glad that it pleased you all. At least I will not have to sit and listen to Targon's stomach making that rumbling noise!"

Matt laughed. He turned his attention to the submersible. "She looks pretty impressive. Do you know when she was used last?"

Sorrol shook his head. "I do not know when it made its last voyage—long before my time, for certain," he replied, looking to the opening door. "I wish you good luck, my friends."

Varl walked in, dressed in a long white robe with a purple sash tied around his wide waist. "Thank you, Sorrol. We'll do our best to bring back Braymar, as well as Matt's computer."

Sorrol shook Varl's hand firmly. "You look good, stranger. If I had not known otherwise, I would say that you were indeed a member of the Noxeran Senate."

Varl rubbed his chin. "Pity my beard hasn't grown just a little more. Then I would have fit in well—and maybe this irritating itching would cease."

"You will pass," replied Sorrol.

"I feel like I should be walking the streets of ancient Rome!" said Varl, loosening the sash.

"You mock, but that is an accurate assessment. What you are wearing is a version of the old Roman toga. Nonius Balbus is obsessed with the Roman Empire and has illusions of grandeur. We are all waiting for the day he declares himself Emperor of Karn! I wish I could be of more assistance to you both, but I fear that nothing will prepare you for what you will encounter."

"You couldn't serve us better than by remaining here with Targon," said Varl softly. "Please look after the boy and monitor our progress in case we run into any difficulty. We'll be indebted to you for that help."

"I am glad to be of assistance." Sorrol turned to Matt. "You also look good," he smiled. "The Noxeran lorica suits you well."

Matt grimaced. "That's what you call it? If you ask me, it's a skirt covered in foil strips. I wouldn't be caught dead in it at home!"

"While I am sure that is true, you would not want to be seen in anything else when you reach Area 6. Besides, be thankful that Balbus did away with the heavy chest plates. How he thinks an army could do battle in this century wearing that garb, I will never understand."

Matt looked up at the young man who had once made him fearful. The wild black hair, deep formal voice and muscular body hid the warmth of Sorrol's personality. Matt shook his hand.

"I hope that you find what you are looking for, young Matt," Sorrol said. "Come back safely."

Varl lifted the long toga high above his feet and carefully stepped off the platform onto the flattened top of the vessel.

Gingerly he walked a few feet along the surface and heaved open the circular hatch. Matt followed. The thick-soled leather boots, tied around his ankles by thongs, felt tight as he took a giant step from the platform onto the submersible. It bobbed slightly in the water, causing him to lose his balance momentarily. He straightened himself, then quickly walked the short distance to the hatch. Matt paused briefly before descending the ladder into the submersible. He waved at Targon and Keela, who peered through the control room window. Targon stared back. Keela smiled feebly and waved. Matt knew they both thought his mission was doomed.

It was hot and dark inside the tiny vessel. Matt could hardly squeeze past Varl to reach the seat behind him. He smoothed back the fringe of the lorica and settled as comfortably as he could. The instrument panels appeared complicated. Flickering colored lights, which showed the systems were in working order, provided the only illumination in the confined space.

In the nose, a circular window granted a glimpse of the outside world. Matt shuddered. Targon had been right—the submersible made him feel claustrophobic. He hoped that Varl had made an accurate assessment of the power system. To die in the submersible was a horrible thought.

Varl put on the headset. "I'll need you to monitor the guidance system," he said, pointing to the keyboard. "I think you'll find the technology slightly advanced but fairly easy to figure out. You're good with computers—let's see how quickly you come to grips with this one."

Matt fiddled with the keys and stared at the small screen

in front of him. Before long the computer was demanding destination coordinates, speed data and depth requirements. Matt pulled a long face and turned to Varl. "I can work the computer fine, but I've no idea what numbers to program into the system."

Varl laughed. He handed Matt a clipboard with the necessary information entered on a chart. "Sorry, this is what you need. Calute had all the information stored in a log from previous trips this craft made."

"How *previous* is that, exactly?"

"About thirty years ago."

"Seriously?" asked Matt. "Don't you think things could have changed in that time?"

"It's possible that the seabed and underwater currents may have shifted slightly, but I estimate any changes would be so marginal that it shouldn't make a difference to the calculations."

"I hope you're right," replied Matt, carefully entering the information into the computer.

"Control Room, we're just about ready here," said Varl to Targon. "Begin flooding the airlock." He could see Targon's anxious face on the screen as Sorrol started the process.

Matt looked up from the computer as the loud noise of swirling, rushing water echoed inside the submersible. He imagined the seawater pouring in through the enormous inlet valve, covering the platform along the edge of the chamber and lapping against the sides of the tiny sub. Matt suddenly felt frightened. He had reached the point of no return. Like it or not, he was on his way to Area 6.

Chapter 7

Marcella's wrist felt bruised and sore. She had been wearing the electronic bracelet for only fifteen minutes, but already it was causing her intense pain. She bit her lip as the pod approached Area 7. The docking mechanism clicked, and the doors slid apart. It had been over a year since she had last had permission to go into the Noxeran half of Karn. Now she was back and even more fearful of her fate.

Tacitus led the group up the stairs and into the corridor. The Karn Elders followed him in silence, their footsteps echoing on the metal grids.

Marcella looked through open doors as they passed by. Before the Noxerans arrived, she had been able to walk freely around this part of Karn. Nothing had changed in fifteen years. The decor was the same, but it felt as though she were in a foreign land. The only difference was the people who walked the corridors and the fear she felt inside. Fifteen years seemed like a lifetime. Would she ever walk freely in this half of Karn again?

As they reached the main sliding doors to the Senate, Tacitus paused and placed a small disc, hanging on a chain from his belt, against a small circular light on the wall. The light blinked briefly and then went out.

"Each of you will raise your bracelet to the light as you

enter. You will be registered as appearing before the Senate and you are required to register again as you depart."

Marcella trembled as her turn approached. Her wrist felt heavy and numb as she lifted the band in position. The light disappeared, and the doors slid open. She stood tall and proud, drew a deep breath, and stepped into the Senate. A large spotlight shone in her eyes, blinding her temporarily.

"Karn, Marcella, Category KF," Tacitus announced with glee into a microphone. Marcella flinched. Categories had not been used as identifying labels in Karn for over two decades. They were degrading. She was sure that the Noxerans had announced categories in an effort to undermine her confidence and humiliate her. She was ushered to a seat by a member of the Senate Guard.

Calute followed her through the doors. Marcella watched his expression change to stone as Tacitus Argus announced, "Karn, Calute, Category KM." He sat down next to Marcella without acknowledging her and stared across the room.

A sea of bearded chins and overweight bodies clothed in white togas faced the ten Karn Elders. Marcella resisted the urge to reposition her hat. Instead she folded her hands tightly in her lap and stared at the front row of arrogant ruddy faces. The atmosphere in the room was hostile even before either side had uttered a sound. There were no smiles and no words of welcome.

"I call this session of the Noxeran Senate to order," announced Tacitus. He bowed before the Princeps, who sat in an ornate wooden chair on a platform in the center of the room, flanked by two senators.

One of the senators hammered a gavel on the table.

Nonius Balbus slowly rose, using the wide arms of his chair to push his heavy frame out of his seat. He placed his right hand across his rounded belly and stood in an arrogant manner befitting a Roman Emperor of centuries past.

Hideous man, thought Marcella. *How pretentious he is.* She studied his swollen mottled cheeks and enormous eyes, which seemed as if they would burst out of their sockets and shoot across the room toward her. An ornate golden crown, tilted slightly to one side, rested on his balding head.

"It is unfortunate and regrettable that I, Princeps Nonius Balbus, have to open this session of the Noxeran Senate," said Balbus, spitting out the last word. "There has been another flagrant abuse of the rules by which we Noxerans have allowed all Karns to remain living here. It has been clearly stated on numerous occasions that no Karn is allowed in Area 6 without Noxeran clearance. We ignored the first two breaches in the hope that they were somehow misunderstandings of the terms of our agreement. When that failed, we tried imprisonment, and finally the threat of death."

He paused to clear his throat and take a quick drink of water. "Now it appears that even death is not a strong enough deterrent! This will not be tolerated any longer!" He banged his fist on the table. "The rules were defined, and the consequences for any individual who chose to break those rules were also made perfectly clear. It is obvious that we have been too lenient."

Calute bravely rose. "Princeps, may I address the Senate?"

"You have one minute to state your case," replied Nonius Balbus without emotion.

Marcella looked at her friend. His expression was serious and his lips quivered. She felt nervous for him.

Calute stood tall. He drew in a deep breath and adjusted his glasses. "As one of the ten Elders of Karn, I place my own life in your hands when I say that I will guarantee that there will be no further breach of the rules as set out by the Noxerans."

"You are either too confident of your ability to control your people or a complete fool," replied Balbus. His face twitched under his left eye. He flicked his head to one side and blinked furiously in irritation as if to hide his imperfection. "Who do you think *you* are that the people of Karn will abide by your promise? Do you think they consider your life sacred? Are you some kind of god?"

Calute hesitated before replying. "All Karns hold each other's lives sacred. I know of no one who would willingly place my life in jeopardy."

"Then you are more of a fool than I thought. This breach of the rules by Braymar is the seventh in the past two years, and this is the fourth promise made to me by one of your Elders. Three Karns languish in our prison as we speak, and three more have lost their lives—and yet you still attempt to offer me words of reassurance? You are no different from the other Elders and can therefore offer no better guarantees!"

"I beg of you, Princeps. Have mercy on my people. It has not been easy for us to relinquish half of The Realm of Karn to the Noxerans."

Nonius Balbus snorted with disgust. "You talk as if this happened yesterday, Elder Calute. We Noxerans have been here *fifteen* years. There is absolutely no excuse!"

"I beg of you to spare the life of Braymar. He is a law-abiding member of Karn and meant no harm."

"Meant no harm?" Balbus laughed loudly. "Are you now naive as well—or do you take *me* for a fool?"

Calute's golden skin showed a hint of red. "I am asking you to spare his life," he added quietly.

Balbus paused for another drink. As he lowered the glass to the table his face twitched again. He shook his head in annoyance and grunted. "Our patience has worn thin. We have already made our decision, and nothing you have said has convinced me to do otherwise."

Calute's legs trembled. He stood in silence while Nonius Balbus spoke quietly, first to the senator on his left and then to the one on his right.

"Our decision remains."

"Braymar is to die?" asked Calute.

Marcella bit her nails in anticipation of the Princeps' reply.

"There are many things worse than death," chuckled Balbus, "and death no longer appears to be a deterrent to you Karns. Braymar will wish he were dead by the time the year is out. By first light tomorrow, you will select five Karns to join Braymar as my personal slaves. They will be permanently shackled, given meager rations and perform heavy laboring tasks. Neither age nor gender is a consideration. If they survive the work set before them, they will *all* be allowed to return to you alive."

"And if they fail?" asked Calute, in shock.

"Then you will send us six more to replace those that

failed. The time for leniency is over. I will finish the geo-thermal project that I came here to complete without any further interference. As punishment for Braymar's tampering with our equipment, more Karns will now suffer the consequences and you will all learn from this ruling." Balbus narrowed his eyes and glared at Calute. "I, Princeps Nonius Balbus, will *not* be made to look a fool, nor will I tolerate those who disobey the laws set by the Senate. Be sure that you select five able-bodied Karns who will represent you well or they will risk the lives of six more."

Calute gulped. "I . . . I . . . beg you . . . to reconsider," he stammered, making one last feeble attempt to reason with his enemy.

Nonius Balbus raised his right eyebrow. "And still you *dare* to bargain with me? Be thankful I am ignoring your foolhardiness!" He banged the gavel down on the table and turned to leave.

"All rise," Tacitus declared. "This session of the Noxeran Senate is closed."

Marcella let out a long breath in relief as the portly senators filed out of the room. She had been so transfixed by the heated proceedings that she had forgotten the pain in her wrists. The Karn Elders began to line up at the door upon the instructions of Tacitus, but Calute remained. He stood motionless, staring at the empty platform.

She took his hand. "You did your best."

"Pity it was not good enough," he whispered. "Thanks to the stubbornness of Braymar, five other Karns may now lose their lives, and our rebellion is as good as over before it has begun. Are we condemned to endure this existence forever?"

*****

Matt watched nervously as the seawater splashed against the window at the front of the submersible. He could see it creeping slowly up the pane of glass. Soon the vessel would be completely underwater.

"How is it going?" asked Targon from the control room.

Matt borrowed the headset and, stretching awkwardly over Varl, moved his face near to the camera so that Targon could see him. Targon looked as anxious as Matt felt.

"So far, so good, I guess," replied Matt. "You're right, though, I feel claustrophobic in here—especially now we're completely submerged." He glanced quickly around the small cabin, expecting to see water seeping through the joints in the welding, but not a drop was visible. The submersible held up well to the pressure of the water on her small frame.

"Good luck," said Targon, "I hope you find your computer."

"Thanks," Matt replied. He removed the headset and handed it back to Varl. "Technology hasn't improved much in this area, has it?"

Varl chuckled. "If you're referring to the time it takes to flood the airlock, I agree." He turned his chair sideways to talk to Matt. "Had the Karns decided to keep the submersible in use, I'm sure they would have devised a quicker method of allowing water into the chamber. If the Realm of Karn had not been pressurized to sea level, departing would have been a lot easier. However, this little vessel has power systems way ahead of your time, and I think you'll be surprised by its maneuverability."

Matt yawned. "How long before the airlock is completely flooded?"

"At a guess, I'd say we're nearly there. Watch for a light to appear on this panel."

"Then what happens?"

"Sorrol will open the outer doors, and we'll be on our way."

A bright red light flickered in the near darkness.

"There she is!" said Varl excitedly, putting the headset back over his ears. "Are you ready, Matt, my boy?"

Matt nodded. "Ready as I'll ever be," he muttered.

"Situation?" Varl asked Targon in the control room. "Okay, we're ready at this end. I'm turning on the power. Sorrol can open the outer doors."

A sound of gurgling water accompanied a creaking of metal. The loud clanging continued for several minutes, and then the enclosure fell silent.

"The doors are open," said Varl, repeating Targon's information to Matt.

The little sub shook momentarily. Then, as if powered by magic, she lifted effortlessly from the floor, and moved silently toward a gaping hole where two solid watertight doors had once formed a wall.

Matt fell silent as Varl maneuvered her through the gap and into the deep.

"Check our bearings," said Varl.

"You're doing great," replied Matt, glancing at the

readings on the screen. "Perfect depth, and the computer says she's following the correct coordinates."

"If we get this right, it will be a short journey. Calute reckoned it would take no more than five minutes."

"Good—the shorter the better! That's about as long as I can take in these cramped conditions."

The movement of the submersible, replicating the swimming pattern of a fish, felt strange. It reminded Matt of a trip he had taken on a hovercraft some years before. The up and down motion of the tiny vessel, combined with a slight tipping from side to side, made him feel nauseous. Matt turned his attention back to the computer and fanned his face with Varl's clipboard in an effort to distract himself.

"Doing okay?" asked Varl.

"Yeah, I'll be fine, thanks."

"As we approach Area 6, we'll switch to manual controls for docking. We have to align correctly in order for the sensor in the submersible's nose to activate the opening and closing of the airlock."

"Understood."

"We're on our way and doing well," said Varl to Targon through the headphones. "Radio silence from here on, just in case the Noxerans are listening on the same frequency. We'll communicate through the keyboard if necessary."

"Can't the Noxerans pick up the transmissions between the computers?" asked Matt.

"Oh, yes—quite easily," said Varl with a knowing smile.

"I don't get it . . ."

Varl took the headset off to explain. "This system is clever. The messages we are sending are encoded within a recording of a whale song. The computer at Targon's end will extract the encoded message and respond in a similar way."

"So if the Noxerans are listening, they will assume they are hearing a school of whales?"

"Correct."

"That's pretty cool."

"No, just technology, my boy!" teased Varl.

Matt could see hundreds of small fish through the window in front. The submersible divided the milling creatures as it carved a path through the shoal and on toward Area 6.

Before long, the craft had left Area 1 behind and progressed round to the side of Area 6. The large metal doors of the airlock were instantly visible. They glinted under the brightness of the huge floodlights, which lit the coral reef.

Varl nudged the vessel slowly toward the entrance and held his breath as he maneuvered the submersible into position. When he was convinced that he had accurately lined up the nose with the center of the doors, he activated the docking sensor in the cone.

Matt watched the airlock doors slowly open until they lay flat against the outer walls. Varl moved the submersible gently into the airlock. He cut the power, allowing it to float gently in and connect with the docking mechanism.

A barely audible 'clunk' signaled success. Varl beamed and patted Matt gently on the back. He waited for the doors to close behind them . . . and waited . . . and waited. After several minutes there was still no movement. Matt frowned, unsure what to expect.

"What's happening?" he whispered.

"Not sure. The airlock outer doors should have closed automatically when we connected with the docking mechanism."

"So what now?" asked Matt, trying to stay calm.

"We can try backing up and re-entering the airlock in the hope that the sensor triggers the docking mechanism."

"Okay, try again."

Varl quietly positioned himself back at the controls, turned on the power, and gently reversed the submersible back out through the doors. He looked at Matt, crossed his fingers and made a second attempt. The vessel clunked back into position, but still nothing happened.

"What now?" Matt asked, a hint of anxiety creeping into his voice.

"I'll check the sensor and the docking trigger in the cone. It'll take a while. Send a message on the computer to Sorrol in the Control Room. Tell them what has happened and that I'm checking the submersible systems."

Matt gave the thumbs-up sign to indicate that he had understood Varl's instructions, and quickly typed the message to Sorrol.

Varl scrambled forward and began to remove a panel. It was hot in the confined space even with the ventilation system running. Matt knew that Varl had a difficult task. It would be hard to distinguish between the various chips under these conditions—particularly when he wasn't totally familiar with how the submersible systems worked. Varl squinted in the low cabin light, removed a few parts and switched them around. He clambered out of the restrictive space and said in a subdued tone, "Can't find anything, but we'll try again."

Matt nodded and watched as Varl repeated the procedure, backing out through the airlock and re-entering in line with the docking mechanism. They waited nervously, but still there was no movement from the doors.

"The submersible sensor worked to open the airlock doors. I suspect the problem is in the docking mechanism itself," said Varl. He reached for the keyboard and typed a message to Sorrol.

We'll have to abandon the mission and return unless you've any idea how we can free the doors.

Sorrol replied within seconds:

Stay put. We will see what we can do from this end.

Varl groaned. "What can they possibly do from there?"

Ten minutes seemed like forever. Even with the emergency ventilation system working, the enclosure had become unbearably hot. There had been no further communication from Area 1. Varl looked depressed. Matt drummed his fingers in a rhythm against the side of his face. He knew that if they failed, finding another way into Area 6 would be virtually impossible. The chances of retrieving his computer were fading fast.

Chapter 8

"**A**ny message from Sorrol?" asked Varl.

Matt looked at the computer screen and shook his head. "Nothing," he said glumly.

Varl sighed. "We'll give it five more minutes and then we'll have to call the whole thing off."

A gentle tapping echoed inside the submersible. Matt sat up abruptly in his seat. He strained his ears and listened for the noise a second time.

"Did you hear that?" he asked Varl.

"I heard something—but what, I'm not sure." Varl swiveled around on his chair and began checking the instrument panels. "There are no warning lights to indicate any malfunctioning systems. Everything seems to be working normally. It must be outside."

"There it is again," whispered Matt. "It's coming from the front."

He directed his eyes to the window. A large object blocked the expanse of glass as it moved past.

"What is *that*?" Matt shouted. His mouth remained wide open. With the lights on inside the submersible it was impossible to see more.

Varl gently placed his hand across Matt's mouth. "Shh! Stay calm and keep quiet." He reached to turn off the lights.

Now they were in the dark with only the faint glow from the computer screen and a few flickering control panel lights.

Matt felt a lump in his throat. His palms became sweaty. He leaned nearer to Varl. In the dark water of the airlock, and without using the submersible's search lights, it was impossible to see farther than a few inches beyond the window. Varl slowly rose from his seat and inched toward the nose of the vessel.

Suddenly a strange figure appeared directly in front of the window. Shapes radiated out like tentacles of a jellyfish, floating and waving with the movement of the water, covering and uncovering the shadowy features. Varl and Matt jumped simultaneously with the sudden shock, the elder man clutching his chest and lurching backwards into Matt.

"*What* is that?" asked Matt, daring to peer from behind Varl's back.

"I think it's a *who*, not a what!" whispered Varl.

"You think someone's swimming at this depth?"

Varl didn't answer. The haunting shape had moved away from the window. They both watched and listened and waited.

"Not positive. But, even a moving human figure can look horrific in the dark of seawater."

"Where do you think he's gone?" muttered Matt.

Varl shrugged. "No idea. This doesn't make sense. No one can swim at this depth without a decompression chamber on hand." His voice trailed off.

"Keela said there was one originally built into Area 6. I saw it on the plans."

"But I'd be surprised if it has been maintained and is still functional."

"She said that she thought it was used by visiting

research scientists just before the Noxerans invaded Karn."

"Then it *could* still be used," Varl said, his bushy eyebrows curling downwards. "It's possible that Noxeran guards heard us arrive and someone has been sent down to investigate. But this airlock is still flooded, so they must have come from one of the other areas and swum around."

"Is that possible?"

"Sure . . . with diving gear. Calute told me that Braymar reported that the guards did not monitor any of the emergency airlocks. I was counting on that information to get us in quietly. Braymar was obviously wrong."

"Perhaps when the Noxerans discovered Braymar's meddling in Area 6, they tightened security."

"I think it's time we got out of here, before reinforcements arrive and we're not dealing with just a lone Noxeran diver," said Varl, settling back at the controls. "Set our return coordinates."

"Done," said Matt, typing in the numbers as fast as his fingers could hit the correct keys.

"Okay, I'll start her up and engage the reverse thrusters." Before Varl could reach for the switch, a hollow groaning sound echoed around them. The small craft swayed slightly in the water. Matt grabbed the edge of the instrument panel for support as the submersible continued to rock and tip.

"Sounds like the outer doors!" Varl groaned. "I think someone's just closed the airlock manually."

"Now we're really trapped, right?" Matt bit his lower lip.

Varl nodded. "There's certainly no way of backing the submersible out now." He slammed his hand down on the control panel in obvious frustration. "We've failed. I blame myself. Calute was right—it was a foolhardy plan in the first place."

"You couldn't have foreseen that this was going to happen," Matt consoled. "We've been unlucky, that's all."

"Luck or not, I allowed us to take a huge risk without well thought-out plans. We should have left here ten minutes ago. Better send a computer message to Sorrol. Tell him we've been discovered and to abort any rescue attempt."

Matt moved toward the computer and began to type, but he had difficulty tearing his eyes away from the level of water descending slowly down the window. He was hardly able to contain his anxiety as it reached the bottom, dreading the moment when the hatch was opened, and he and Varl were hauled out. His hands shook as he typed the message.

"Perhaps we can fool them," said Matt, his voice quaking. He looked at his uncomfortable clothing. "You never know, we might just pass as Noxerans!"

Varl smiled. "Matt, the optimist," he chuckled. "That's what I like about you, my boy—always ready to try anything and always thinking on the positive side."

"Well, we might as well be ready to talk our way out of this," said Matt, trying to push in front.

"Hang on there!" Varl grabbed two of the strips on Matt's lorica and pulled him back to his seat. "Let's be careful. Best be prepared." He removed a small hand-held cylinder that Sorrol had given to him from one of the overhead storage compartments. "I'll go first. You stay well back—do you hear?"

"What's that?"

"A stunner. According to Sorrol it releases a powerful

electrical charge that will put an attacker to sleep long enough for us to make a hasty exit."

"What good will that do?" asked Matt. "We'll have nowhere to run to—Noxeran guards will be everywhere."

"It might buy us a little time," said Varl, concealing the slender canister behind his back.

The lever on the airlock above them moved slightly. Matt held his breath. The lever turned again. His legs quivered. Finally, there was a loud clunk, and then the heavy circular hatch opened. He felt like a caged animal. Light shone down through the opening. Matt squinted to see his captor, his eyes taking time to adjust from the gloom of the submersible. Suddenly, a head of long wet hair peered down through the hatch.

"Are you both okay?" asked a soft voice.

"Keela, what the . . .?" said Matt, staring up at her jubilant smile. He felt the tension in his muscles subside, and found himself breathing freely for the first time since they had entered the airlock.

"Pleased to see me, I hope?" she giggled.

"You bet!" said Matt.

Varl regained his composure. "I don't understand—how did you get here? We thought that you said there was only one remaining submersible!"

"And there *is* only one . . ." Keela replied.

"Then how did you get here?" Varl strained his neck upward.

Keela grabbed her hair into a thick bunch and wrung it out like a twisted towel. The released water fell from the hatch above and collected at Matt's feet. She clambered down the metal ladder, her clothes dripping, and jumped awkwardly off the last rung. Matt's attention was immediately diverted to Keela's bare feet, which landed heavily in the puddle that had formed on the floor. He stared in disbelief. Not only were they significantly larger than his own, but she had no toes! Instead, large webbed ends, which opened and closed in front of his eyes, seemed to be at home in the small pool of water on the floor.

"You're . . . you've . . . you've got . . ." he stammered.

Varl followed Matt's gaze. His jaw dropped.

"I swam," she replied simply. "You can see that my feet make it easy."

"Your feet? But . . . how? You've no air tanks!" said Varl, looking totally shocked by her revelation. "And you don't appear to have suffered with decompression sickness."

Matt finally found his tongue. Fear crept back into his bones as he asked her the ultimate question. "Are you an . . . an . . . android?" He waited for her response with mixed emotions.

"No, I am *not* an android," she replied indignantly, "—and no, I am not human either. I am simply a Karn." She smiled as if her words explained everything easily.

Varl scratched his chin. "A Karn? I think *that* perhaps requires further explanation, my dear," he said, maintaining a scientific tone. "What exactly *is* a Karn apart from one who *lives* in Karn?"

"This is the secret of the Karn people. We are the product of Dr. Willard Karn's genetic engineering on humans."

"Oh, my!" said Varl with a broad grin, his inquisitive

nature taking over. "This I've got to hear!"

"Well, I understand your shock and need for answers, but further explanation will have to be saved for later," Keela reminded him. "We are all at risk while we stand idly talking. The mission has been saved for now. You had better continue as planned. If I am right, the light above the airlock door now shines green and a Noxeran guard could enter at any time."

"Yes, you're right of course. Let's get on with it, Matt, my boy," said Varl eagerly. "Switch off the power and pass me the leather pack. Let's go and fix the airlock warning light before we're in more trouble."

Matt turned to the computer monitor. In capital letters a message from Sorrol read:

SORRY TOO LATE. HELP ALREADY ON ITS WAY.

"Pity they didn't send us this message sooner! Could have saved us both a lot of panic!" Matt lamented.

"We did not want to get your hopes up in case I had trouble with the manual door mechanism," said Keela. "Besides, would you have believed Sorrol if he had told you what I was intending to do?"

"Probably not . . . but thanks, Keela." Varl threw the satchel around his neck, rubbed his hands together, and began to climb the metal rungs of the ladder. "You saved the day—even if you almost gave me a heart attack in the process!" he shouted back as he neared the top.

"Please go carefully," she responded.

"What will you do while we are gone?" Matt asked her, hesitating on the bottom rung.

"I will have to stay here—you will need me to open the

airlock doors again. I will make sure that I am out of sight and I will go underwater if need be. The base water level of the airlock is at ten feet, as it is in Area 1—plenty of expanse for me to disappear into in an emergency."

Matt followed Varl up the ladder. He paused at the top. "We'll be back with Braymar, you'll see!"

* * * * *

Matt watched Varl tread carefully along the top of the submersible. The dark ten feet of remaining water lapped gently against the hull. Keela had turned on two small spotlights, which barely illuminated the area. Lifting his robe above his knees, Varl jumped onto the platform. He skidded slightly on the wet surface as he landed. Matt tried not to laugh.

"Noxeran sandals!" Varl muttered. "There's no grip on the soles. Couldn't Balbus have thought of something better to wear?"

Matt caught up with him. "At least the Roman soldiers wore boots with thicker soles," he commented, as he leaped easily alongside the older man. "But you'd think that after two thousand years, the Noxerans could have done better with modernizing both designs."

Varl grinned. "Now let's get serious. We've a task to complete and I'd like to do it successfully. Time is already against us."

They approached the door at the end of the platform. Matt stared at the large red letters stamped in the center: 'Area 6 – DANGER.' It was the same lettering that he had seen when he first landed in Karn. Through a small glass circle he could see into the corridor on the other side.

Varl placed his satchel on the floor and squinted through. "All clear, I think. Of course I can't see directly on either side of the door."

"Let's hope Calute was right when he said that there was no central monitoring system of the emergency airlocks," said Matt, crossing his fingers.

"That was years ago. We just have to hope that the Noxerans didn't see the need to install new equipment." Varl opened the satchel. He pulled out a few items and spread them on the ground.

Matt glanced at his watch. "It's been at least fifteen minutes since Keela drained the airlock and we've seen no sign of anyone."

"That's exactly as we expected," said Varl, ferreting in his bag for more tools. "Even if this part of Area 6 is normally patrolled, with the arrival of the Karn Elders for the Senate meeting the guards should have been diverted to Area 7. Calute reckoned we'd have at least four hours to do the job and get out again."

Matt looked at his watch again. "That means we've got less than three hours left."

"Okay, I'm ready to start. Our first task is to deactivate the green light above the door on the other side and make sure that the red light is permanently illuminated."

"What are the lights for?"

"Red shows that the outer doors are open and the airlock is full of water; green shows they are closed and that the airlock has been drained. We don't want anyone coming in here to investigate and finding the submersible."

"So that's why you've got to get rid of the green light and keep the red light showing," said Matt.

"Exactly. The door into Area 6 automatically locks when the airlock is full of water. If the red light is on, I hope no one will even attempt to open the door."

"Clever," said Matt. "Can you do it?"

"An easy rewiring procedure," said Varl confidently. "Our main problem is that the circuitry panel is located on the other side of this door in full view of anyone who might pass by."

"Just great! Nothing is ever easy, is it?"

"Here, take this," said Varl, handing him the stunner. "I can do the job in less than five minutes, but you'll have to stand guard at the end of the corridor. Ready?"

Matt looked him in the eyes. "Sure," he replied, less than confidently.

Varl forced the sealing mechanism open and heaved the watertight door ajar. He motioned to Matt to help him. The door was thick and heavy. It took both of them to push it fully back and swing it closed after.

Matt crept down the corridor. The overlapping lightweight strips on his lorica swung back and forth. He cursed the outfit as he continued to the corner and peered around the edge. The distant sound of boots resounded on the mesh flooring of the corridor. Matt listened intently for a few seconds. There could be no doubt, a Noxeran guard was heading in their direction.

Matt dived back against the wall. His heart pounded. He rubbed his clammy hands together, frantically searching for a quick solution. How could he possibly warn Varl in time?

Chapter 9

"**O**ne hour! Just one hour!" Marcella complained as they left the pod chute and walked toward the Elders' Chamber. "I cannot believe that is all it took! No debate. . .no discussion—just doling out the punishment and treating us like scum! Even to the point where they announced our categories as we entered the Senate. How degrading!" She massaged her wrists gently. "I hope I never lay eyes on that despicable man again."

Calute walked solemnly beside her. He had no words of comfort on this occasion. "I feared that the Noxerans would be harsh in their judgment, but this was worse than I had anticipated. Nonius Balbus behaved true to Noxeran form. The category system was abolished decades ago. I am sure that Balbus instructed Tacitus to use it to humiliate us all before the Senate proceedings began."

"Nonius Balbus—huh! Such a pretentious name. And slavery? That is just taking his Roman obsession too far. Next he will be conquering kingdoms and declaring himself Emperor of the World!"

"Let us pray that never happens. Now we have to concentrate on selecting five Karns who will almost certainly be giving up their lives," Calute growled. "What a grim task."

"And what of the old man, Varl, and the boy? We guaranteed them four hours with no guards while we had our meeting with the Noxeran Senate. We have only been able to give them one."

"I know. I worry for their safety. They may have found their way into Area 6, but getting out now that the pass system has been changed will be difficult."

"That is certainly an understatement!" Marcella said with tears in her eyes. "Impossible, if you ask me."

Calute paused at the door to the Elders' chamber. "This will not be easy," he said. "It is one of the hardest tasks that has ever faced us as the governing body of the people of Karn. Did you manage to get a message to Sorrol?"

Marcella brushed away the tears. "Yes, and I pray that he has succeeded. So, let us be strong and hope that the Elders make the *right* decision." She took a deep breath and stood tall.

Calute held up his identification chip to the pad on the wall. They stepped between the opening doors of the Elders' Chamber in a dignified manner and with heads held high.

Most of the other Elders were already seated around the huge table. Sorrol, to Marcella's relief, stood quietly in the far corner. He smiled at her, which gave her hope. She looked around the table at her friends and colleagues. The room was silent, and grim faces stared at them as they took their seats.

Odenna, one of the older Elders, rose slowly. She was well respected, but frail.

"You did more than any of us could have asked, Calute. We thank you for your courage in speaking to Balbus and the Senate, but this is a task that none of us wish to have a hand in," she said in a shaky voice.

Calute's mouth dropped open. "And you think that Marcella and I will enjoy having to select five of our people to go to an almost certain death?"

Odenna avoided Calute's eyes. She shook her head and looked down at the table. "I am not saying that you will. But we should not *have* to make such a horrendous decision."

Marcella felt the anger rise up inside her. "And if we do not, what do you think will happen? I will tell you . . . we will *all* be at the mercy of the Noxeran Senate. Legionaries will be sent to storm our half of Karn. They will take five Karns by force—or perhaps more as punishment for our disobedience! Women, children, the elderly . . . what will the Noxerans care? Is that what you all wish to see happen?"

Odenna sat down in silence.

"Well?" shouted Marcella. "Why do you not answer, any of you? Either we make the choice, horrendous as it is, or they will make it for us."

Larkin pushed back his chair and stood determinedly. His thin face showed little emotion as his beady eyes focused on Marcella. Marcella prepared herself to listen because he often had something profound to say.

"Could there not be another option?" he asked.

"Such as?" Marcella responded.

"Before Braymar was captured, we were close to completing a plan to rid Karn of the Noxerans. Can this still not be done without Braymar?"

Marcella, unfamiliar with the details of the plan, turned to Calute to answer.

"We needed several more months in order to guarantee success, and Braymar is the key," he began. "It is he who has a detailed knowledge of Noxeran schedules, their underwater project, machinery, and rotation of guards. No record was kept for fear that the Noxerans might uncover the plan. I do not see how we could consider going ahead when so much knowledge is now lacking."

"Are you telling me that our entire plan hinged upon Braymar?" snorted Larkin.

"I am afraid so," replied Calute. "There are a few others who have helped Braymar and have limited knowledge, but they do not know enough."

"Then we have learned another valuable lesson here today," said Larkin, sitting down in disgust. "Let us not make the mistake of creating one hero in the future!"

"I agree," said Calute. "We made a grave mistake in assigning the task to one Karn. However, there is currently another plan in the works."

Marcella flashed a fiery warning at Calute. She knew where he was heading. Surely he would not tell the Elders about Varl and the boys. How could he give the Elders hope when the time travelers were almost certainly in trouble, too?

Calute ignored her frown. "You may remember that Marcella and I have been helping three time travelers who landed in Karn several days ago. They lost their method of getting back to their own time—a small computer—and are currently attempting to retrieve it from Area 6."

"And how will this help us in any way? If anything, it might make matters worse!" snapped Larkin.

"Because they are also attempting to rescue Braymar as we speak," said Calute proudly.

The chamber erupted in excited chatter. The Elders

suddenly seemed more relaxed, and a few faces even bore the traces of a smile. Calute cleared his throat loudly, and the talking finally ceased.

"Tell us more," said Larkin, eagerly awaiting an explanation.

"I am only prepared to say this much," replied Calute. "The time travelers are risking their lives to help us. They used the distraction of the Elders' visit to the Senate to gain access to the Noxeran half. We should know if they have succeeded in the next six hours."

Loud talking again filled the room. Marcella felt angry that Calute had given the Elders hope where hope perhaps did not exist, but she understood his reasoning and decided to use it to their advantage.

"Friends, you can see that all is not lost." She smiled and waited for their attention. The talking died. "But hard as it is, we must make an alternative plan in case our new friends fail." A more serious air returned to the room. "I think that you will find that we have an acceptable solution."

Sorrol stepped forward from the corner where he had been waiting patiently to speak. "I thank Marcella and Calute for allowing me into the Chamber to be part of this discussion. I wish to offer myself as one of the chosen five. I do this gladly to serve the Realm of Karn, and I know of others who are also prepared to take this challenge." He handed Marcella a piece of paper with a list of names.

There was stunned silence.

"Challenge?" said Odenna in horror. "I hardly think it is that. You are offering us your life."

"Indeed, but better I die than a child or a mother. I am

young and physically fit. It is obvious that I would stand a better chance at surviving what the Noxerans require of me."

"Thank you, Sorrol," said Marcella. "We are all indebted to you and the others who have volunteered. We hope that if our time traveler friends return with Braymar before tomorrow morning, you will not have to go."

"Does any member of the Meeting of Elders have an objection to this proposal?" asked Calute. He studied each and every face at the table. No one spoke. "Then it is agreed. I declare the meeting of Elders at a close. We will meet again at seven tomorrow morning. Let us hope that the new day brings better news."

* * * * *

Matt could hear the guard approaching. He held the stunner tightly in his hand. It would have to be his last resort. He tucked it into his belt, behind his back, and within easy reach in an emergency. Varl continued to work on the rewiring. Aside from shouting down the corridor to warn him, there was no way Matt could attract the old man's attention. Matt had a major decision to make. Either he could risk being caught, but allow Varl the opportunity to succeed on his own, or he could warn Varl and hope that they could both find a way out of the situation. He looked down the corridor one last time. Varl still had his back to him and continued to work diligently. Without really knowing what he would say or do, Matt boldly stepped around the corner to face the enemy.

The Noxeran guard seemed stunned by the sudden appearance of a teenage boy. He came to an abrupt halt and eyed Matt suspiciously, scanning the boy's garments from his footwear to his lorica. The guard's right hand firmly clutched a programmable vidium, which was clipped in a harness attached to a heavily studded belt.

Matt stared at the short black weapon. Calute had warned him about the vidium. Balbus enjoyed standing before the Senate and dressing in updated Roman attire, but at weaponry he had seen sense and drawn the line. In 2540 a more sophisticated defense against an enemy was needed. Matt dared not think about the power that this technical device might wield. He racked his memory for the key words and formal language of the Noxerans that Marcella had taught him.

"Greetings, fellow legionary," Matt began in a loud voice, hoping that the sound would carry around the corner and down the corridor to Varl. "I appear to have lost my way and need directions."

The legionary's eyes narrowed as he took time to think about the request. "What is your name, boy?" he asked in a gruff tone.

Matt felt his knees quiver slightly. "Marcus," he quickly responded.

"I have not heard of you before—nor have I seen you before," the legionary replied.

"That is because I arrived yesterday," said Matt, hardly believing his own audacity.

"I do not recall that yesterday was the day for a legionary shift change. You look too young to be a legionary! Show me your identification chip." He unsnapped his holster and pointed the vidium at Matt.

Without flinching, Matt found himself shouting and declaring, "I am the nephew of Princeps Nonius Balbus, and you dare to threaten me? I do not think my uncle would be pleased to hear of this in-depth interrogation by one of his legionaries."

The legionary immediately took a step backward, red-faced and taken aback by the boy's proclamation. He bowed his head. "I ask for your forgiveness, young sir. I am honored to be in the presence of one so noble."

"Your apology is accepted," replied Matt in a condescending tone. He waved his hand in a regal manner befitting the nephew of a Princeps. "Tell me *your* name."

"Uh, um . . . my name is Argus," he stammered, "—but I beg of you not to report this incident to your uncle. I meant no disrespect to his nephew."

Matt felt a hand rest squarely upon his shoulder. He froze momentarily, his mind racing, his heart pounding against his chest cavity and his sudden burst of bravery wavering. If a second legionary was now on the scene, he was in serious trouble and his charade would not work. He stared at the legionary's vidium still out of its holster and then turned his head slowly to face the new threat to his already precarious situation.

Varl stood directly behind. He had a broad grin across his face, which told Matt that the rewiring had been successfully completed. Matt smiled back, trying not to show his relief in a way that would make Argus suspicious. Better still, Varl's presence would help convince the guard.

"Argus, may I present my guardian and teacher, Senator Varl."

"I am honored to meet you, Senator Varl," said Argus, dipping his head and lowering his eyes.

Varl bowed accordingly. A faint smile crept into the corner of his mouth, indicating an appreciation of Matt's ingenuity and quick thinking. Now was not the time to allow a smile or a laugh to give their game away. Matt quickly turned back to Argus.

"I will not report this matter to my uncle if you will kindly direct me and my guardian to the vault."

"The vault?" Argus visibly gulped. "What . . .?" he spluttered, and then apparently thought better than to interrogate the boy a second time. "I must get clearance from my commander first."

Varl placed his arm around Argus' shoulders. "We have a small problem. You see, Marcus is in a bit of a predicament," he whispered into the legionary's ear. "The Princeps gave him a new computer upon his arrival yesterday—the latest design—and the boy has already misplaced the treasured item! Another legionary has told him that it was found and placed in the vault. Marcus is anxious to find the computer before his uncle discovers how neglectful he has been of such a valuable gift. I am sure that you understand the sensitive nature of this request. The fewer people who know about this, the better. The boy will be indebted to you."

The legionary said nothing for a minute. Varl waited patiently. Matt held his breath.

"I will be honored to help you out in return for your kindness to me," Argus finally replied. "I will take you to the vault room, but you will have to deal with the commanding vault guard yourself. There will be nothing that I can say that will convince him to open the vault without higher authority."

Argus strode proudly down the corridor leading the way. Varl winked at Matt as they followed behind.

"Marcus and Senator Varl?" Varl mouthed. "*What* do you call that?"

Matt smirked. "Quick thinking," he whispered back.

His imagination and resourcefulness had got them out of a tight situation . . . for now. The next step would not be so easy.

Chapter 10

Argus raised his identification chip to the wall pad and the doors to the vault room slid smoothly apart. Varl stepped over the threshold and into a brightly lit room. A raised narrow walkway divided the expanse in two. He had imagined the vault would be behind enormous sealed doors, with an elaborate locking mechanism, or with a vast array of lasers designed to deter those who might consider entering. Instead, the vault room was partitioned into large sections completely open to the walkway. The contents were on display for all to see.

Each section was stacked with weaponry of varying sizes and types, explosives, devices that Varl could not identify and finally, ingots of gold. It seemed too easy for anyone to enter and help himself. And where were the guards to oversee such a valuable cache?

Matt turned in a full circle, studying the amazing exhibition. Varl could guess what was going through the boy's mind. What would prevent them from stunning Argus immediately and walking into any section of the vault to look for Matt's computer?

Within seconds, a vault guard appeared from a small cubicle at the opposite end of the walkway. He approached Argus, vidium in hand. "How can I be of assistance?" he asked in a gruff voice.

Argus briefly explained the situation and then turned to face Varl. "This is Commander Carella. I will leave you in his hands, Senator Varl and young Marcus. I am afraid I can do no more."

"Thank you." Varl bowed his head lightly. "Your help will be remembered."

Varl watched the vault room doors slide closed behind Argus. "I hope that you clearly understand the situation, Commander Carella—this is a very delicate matter," he said in a tone of authority. "Marcus *must* find his computer. We all wish to spare the boy the wrath of our good leader, his uncle, the Princeps."

Carella stared at Varl, his face expressionless. He raised his vidium and waved it around in a threatening manner. Matt recoiled at the closeness of the weapon.

"I hope that *you* understand, Senator Varl, that this matter is beyond my help. I have no ability to open *any* section of the vault." Carella grinned at the obvious discomfort of his visitors and continued to point his vidium directly at Varl's chest.

"Open?" Varl found himself saying, undeterred by Carella's aggressive stance. He looked again at the vault contents—seemingly available, right in front of him.

"Uh . . . I should say, deactivate the sonic wall," clarified Carella.

"Oh . . . of course . . . *the sonic wall* has to be deactivated," said Varl, staring at the open sections for some indication of what this would mean to an intruder. Nothing was blatantly visible. "And who *does* have the ability?"

"First you must get written permission from one of the

two centurions. Then it will take two of three commanding vault guards to enter their codes into the computer at the same time. I have access to only one half of the necessary digits that complete the vault combination."

"Two *commanding* guards simultaneously, eh?" repeated Varl. He looked toward the walls of the guard cubicle, wondering how many regular guards might be found on duty at one time under each commander. He thought he had heard other voices during their conversation.

"I am afraid so." Carella smiled wryly. "The system was cleverly designed. There is no way around the procedure . . . and no way to cross the sonic wall."

Varl grinned back, realizing that for now they were defeated. He had to find out more about sonic walls and about how many vault guards to expect at one time. Now was not the time to play hero and make a hasty attempt.

"I don't think that will be necessary," he replied. "We will get the required permission and return. I just hope that this poor boy will be able to retrieve the valuable gift before his uncle is aware of the situation."

Carella's facial expression softened. "I am sorry that I cannot help the young man. I will call Centurion Anthony and tell him to expect you. He is a very trustworthy Noxeran and I am sure that he will keep your confidences." He finally lowered the vidium to his side.

"Thank you, Carella," said Varl politely. "Any help you can give will gladly be accepted."

There was a loud cough from the guard cubicle. An elderly figure stepped out from behind the low walls.

"That won't be necessary, Carella. I will take them to see

the centurion," the man said confidently.

Varl's head pounded with the stress. The situation was getting out of hand. He had not anticipated this outcome—yet another Noxeran involved in their quest for Matt's computer. He strained to see over Carella's shoulder at the vault guard who approached them. He was not dressed as the other legionaries, but as a senator. The man's gray hair was tied back neatly in a ponytail, and his long silvery beard had a pointed straggly end. Varl studied the familiar features. Could it be? Surely not! Matt's mouth was open wide. Had Matt recognized the thin figure with the radiant smile?

"Thank you, Senator Gallus. It is lucky that you were here to check our store cupboard," said Carella, relieved to be free of the problem.

"Indeed it was," replied Gallus with twinkling eyes. "Come, my friends, let me be of assistance and allow our good friend to return to his duties."

Carella placed his vidium back in its holster and walked back to the guard cubicle. Varl and Matt followed the senator silently through the vault room doors and into the corridor.

The moment that they were on their own, Matt whispered, "Dorin, my friend from Zaul, is it really you?"

"Sshh! Not here!" Dorin replied. "It's too risky. Quick, follow me."

* * * * *

Matt and Varl accompanied Dorin a short way down the corridor and up a narrow flight of stairs to a second level.

Dorin paused at the top, checked the open area beyond, and led them across the mesh floor to one of many locked doors on the other side.

"In here," he muttered, raising his identification chip to the wall pad. He ushered them into a tiny storeroom. As the door closed, the light turned on automatically. Dorin threw open his arms and hugged first Matt and then Varl, pounding his friends heartily on the back.

Tears welled in his eyes. "Zang it! I can't believe my luck!" he cried. "I thought I was here on my own, and that I had left Zaul forever. Where *did* you two spring from?"

"It's a long story," replied Varl. "But I'm impressed. What was it you said to that guard?"

"Let me be of assistance and allow our good friend to return to his duties," said Matt, lowering his voice and imitating Dorin's posture and expressions. He was delighted to have found his elderly friend.

Dorin laughed loudly. "I quickly had to learn the phrases and formal way of speaking so they wouldn't realize I was not a Noxeran."

Varl shook his hand. "Well you definitely succeeded, and now we need your help again. We can all get out of here, if we can find a way to open the vault and retrieve Matt's computer."

"What makes you think it's in the vault?" Dorin asked.

"We're just guessing," said Varl, "—but it seems the most likely place the Noxerans would put it for safekeeping."

"That's assuming they found it in the first place," said Dorin, winking.

"What are you implying?" asked Varl.

"I'm saying that the Noxerans never had Matt's computer—*I* did!" He reached behind some boxes on a high shelf and produced the recognizable black laptop with the cracked lid.

"Wow!" shrieked Matt. "I don't believe it!" He grabbed the computer out of Dorin's grasp and ran his hands lovingly over the surface of his most treasured possession. This was too good to be true. "Thanks, Dorin."

"I mysteriously found myself here—on the floor of this storeroom, with your computer by my side. Fortunately I had the good sense to hide it before I ventured beyond the door."

"Did the Noxerans interrogate you when they caught you?" Matt asked.

Dorin shook his head. "Strange, and very lucky, that I dress like the Noxeran senators. The arrival of new guards and senators from the mainland coincided with me turning up here. Before I knew it, I had luxurious accommodation and even a job." He dangled the identification chip in front of them. "It was assumed that I was in charge of restocking supplies and equipment when I was seen leaving this room. I just kept busy and tried to look like I knew what I was doing. My greatest problem has been reading the labels on all of these boxes!" Dorin frowned and drew in a deep breath. Deep lines creased his brow as he stared at Matt. "Say, how *did* I come to be in Noxera, and how did you come to be dressed as you are?" He pursed his lips anxiously, waiting for the reply.

"Noxera? This is Karn, actually," said Matt, knowing that his answer would bring more questions.

Dorin looked totally confused as if it wasn't the answer he

anticipated.

Varl laughed. "Don't worry, we'll fill you in on the details later. We've all asked the same question about how we got here, and how we wish we knew! Matt's computer still holds the answers. So, what are you waiting for, Matt? Open it up and let's see what it tells you this time," said Varl, eagerly settling himself on the floor.

Matt sat down next to him and crossed his legs. He hesitated. His heart raced. "What if the battery's dead?"

"It's not," said Dorin sheepishly. "I have a confession to make. I haven't told you the complete truth." He fell silent for a minute. "I first found myself in the Forbidden Hall in Zaul. I could hear the Protectors coming. Matt's computer was by my side but I couldn't see Matt anywhere. I was terrified. I hoped the boy's computer might somehow save me and send me back to my room—so I opened the lid."

"What happened?" asked Matt.

"After a few seconds there was a bright purple screen and one word flashed across it." Dorin turned red with embarrassment. "I wish I could have read that word. Then bright lights flickered and little blue boxes ran across the screen vertically and horizontally. They were fast, so very fast. They mesmerized me."

"Neverlost!" shouted Matt. "That's the Neverlost program kicking in."

"Care to explain?" asked Varl.

"It's a file recovery program on my laptop."

"Ah!" Varl nodded his head indicating he understood. "Then what happened, Dorin?"

"I was frightened by what I saw on the screen next."

"Frightened by what you saw?" Varl questioned. "What exactly *did* you see?"

Dorin bit his lip. "I *really* must learn to read. I saw more strange words appear in gray rectangular boxes in the center of the screen and then . . ." He paused. His face looked pale.

"Then . . .?" goaded Matt.

"Then I saw pictures of a huge dark-haired being with a golden face. He looked extremely angry. There were people strapped into seats that seemed to be moving fast through a tube. Their faces shook so violently they looked as if they might explode. I thought they were all going to die so I closed the lid quickly. Thick swirling clouds surrounded me. I couldn't breathe. I remember choking and fighting for air. Suddenly I was out of the Forbidden Hall and here on the floor of the storeroom, still with Matt's computer. I was so scared by what I had seen on the screen that I hid it behind those boxes and haven't touched it since."

Matt was delighted by Dorin's tale. He placed his hand gently on the old man's arm. "I think I know what has happened, and why we are all here."

"You do?" said Dorin.

"I have a vague idea from what I've heard," said Varl, "and I don't think I'm going to like your explanation, Matt, my boy, because it will disprove my time travel theory yet again."

"By opening my computer when he did, Dorin may just have saved me from the Protectors!"

Dorin's color returned to his cheeks. "I did?"

"The little blue boxes Dorin described are part of something called Neverlost, which has the ability to recover programs. Let me search the computer log and see if we can pull up the computer's recent activity." Matt tapped on the keys for a minute or two. Dorin and Varl watched silently. "Here we go," said Matt, grinning happily. "These are the words that appeared on the screen."

This computer was shut down incorrectly. 'Neverlost' will attempt to recover your program. Recovery attempt commencing. Please wait.

What does it say?" asked Dorin.

Matt read the sentences aloud and drummed his fingers on the lid of his laptop to pass the time.

Recovery successful. Neverlost has recovered your program and will restart it immediately.

Just as I thought," said Matt excitedly. "Neverlost recovered the *Keeper of the Kingdom* information and restarted my game."

"Then why did we continue playing the game in Zaul?" asked Varl.

"We had to," said Matt, "—until Neverlost had finished scanning the memory and the program recognized our game results."

Matt scrolled further through the log, pulling up the information that Dorin had been unable to read. Varl read the words out loud.

Congratulations! You have successfully completed Level 1 of *Keeper of the Kingdom*. Welcome to Level 2, *Keeper of the Realm*. Good Luck!

Matt's eyes lit up. "See, I *was* right," he announced. "We *are* still playing my game. *Keeper of the Realm* is Level 2!"

Varl scratched his head. "So you think that we've been playing Level 2 of your *Keeper of the Kingdom* game ever since Dorin activated Neverlost in the Forbidden Hall and propelled us all into Karn?"

Matt nodded. "It makes perfect sense. He did have his hands on the lid of my computer when I entered the final commands of Level 1 in his room."

"So what has become of our friends back in Zaul?" asked Dorin, with fear in his voice.

"Well, the program says that we successfully completed Level 1 of my game—so I can only presume that everyone is safe, and that Zaul is still free of the Keeper and of the Protectors."

Dorin sighed with relief, the color returning to his cheeks. "So we *do* have a free Zaul to return to."

Varl chuckled. "And I really believed we were time traveling with you. Now you are trying to convince me yet again that we are playing a child's computer game?"

"Is this not the *Realm* of Karn? When I arrived in Karn, didn't I first meet Sorrol, a huge dark-haired man with a golden complexion, just as Dorin saw on the screen? Haven't we all experienced the pod chutes where we were strapped into seats and propelled so fast that our bodies shook violently—just as Dorin described?"

"Okay, Matt, my boy, I'm convinced—well, almost," said Varl.

Chapter 11

"**I** presume that we are still playing by the same rules as in Level 1?" asked Varl.

"I think so," replied Matt, staring at the computer screen. "We have to eliminate the Keeper and free the people of Karn to win the game."

Varl scratched the side of his head vigorously. "Now the question is: who is the Keeper of Karn?"

"Princeps, Nonius Balbus, perhaps?" Dorin suggested.

Varl grunted. "Seems too easy an answer, if you ask me."

"We also need to work out *how* to free the people of Karn," added Matt.

"Well, my boy, what are you waiting for? I think you'd better find the game instructions for Level 2," suggested Varl.

Matt pulled up the *'Menu'* and read the words out loud for Dorin's benefit. "I've clicked on *'Rules'*," he announced, scrolling down a list of options. "Here we are. *'Number 4, Freedom Fighters'*—that seems to be what we want."

The sound of beating drums accompanied pictures of the vault room. The screen zoomed in on the guard cubicle and finally on a vidium held by a legionary.

"A now familiar place," muttered Varl, "and one I assume we are going back to?"

"What does it say?" asked Dorin as the riddle appeared on the screen.

A deep eerie voice read the rhyme.

In Level 2, rules stay the same
Destroy the Keeper to win the game
Freedom Fighters hold the key
To rid the realm of slavery
Free the leader of this clan
Inventive but careful with your plan
Best laid schemes are known to fail
Loyalty and teamwork will prevail.

Varl shook his head. "Yet another poetic riddle. I was hoping that Level 2 of your game might be different."

"No. Each level of a computer game has similar elements. We managed to work out the verses in Level 1—I'm sure we can do the same with this one," said Matt, closing the computer lid. "I'm conserving the battery again."

"Don't worry about that, my boy," said Varl. "When we return to Karn we'll find a way to charge up your pack."

"Do you understand the meaning of the rhyme?" asked Dorin.

Matt stretched his legs out in front of him. He had been sitting on the floor of the small storeroom for over thirty minutes, totally involved in his computer and the intense conversation. Now his feet began to tingle with the lack of circulation. He got to his feet and rubbed his calves vigorously while answering Dorin's question.

"Well, this one seems pretty easy. We've heard of the Freedom Fighters. Braymar, whom we came here to rescue, leads the plot against Nonius Balbus. If the Freedom

Fighters hold the key, and we have to free the leader, I guess we continue with the plan to get Braymar out of here."

Varl scratched his unshaven chin. "Don't know how you cope with a beard," he muttered to Dorin. "I think Matt is right. Finding Braymar and getting him back safely should be our first priority."

"I've heard of this man, Braymar," said Dorin.

Varl stood up and helped the old man to his feet. "According to Calute, he's being held prisoner in Area 8."

Dorin leaned back against the shelving and folded his arms across his chest. "Sorry, but you're wrong. Prison guards moved him to the vault room a few hours ago."

"The vault room? Are you sure?" gasped Matt.

"Positive. I was checking the prison stores and watched the guards escort him."

"But why the vault room?" Matt queried.

"For greater security. There's some important Senate meeting taking place," replied Dorin. "I overheard the guards talking."

"It's the meeting with the Karn Elders," Varl informed. "It's our diversion to get in and out of here."

"The Noxerans didn't seriously think we would try and free Braymar during the meeting, did they?" said Matt.

"Well, my boy, isn't that exactly what we had in mind after locating your computer?" Varl chuckled.

Matt grinned at him. "You're right, of course. But why the vault room? How can that be more secure than the prisons in Area 8?"

"Because they put him inside the vault," replied Dorin.

"*Inside* the vault?" said Matt incredulously.

"Correct—*inside* the vault. I was curious after I heard the conversation in Area 8. So I used the excuse of checking supplies to get into the vault room."

"But we didn't see him . . . and there was no sign of any extra guards," said Matt, still having a hard time understanding the reasoning behind this unexpected turn of events.

"You couldn't see the whole vault from where you were standing. There are sections in rows behind."

"And I bet that all sections have sonic walls," Varl interrupted, "and there are no sonic walls in Area 8."

Dorin smiled. "You're always one step ahead, Varl. The Area 8 prison complex was built as part of the original Realm of Karn one hundred and fifty years ago. The prison is outdated and the guards always complain about the risky security."

"So the sonic wall system was brought here recently by the Noxerans?" questioned Matt.

"I would imagine so," Varl answered, his forehead furrowed in thought. "It therefore makes sense that they would move Braymar to a more secure location, which causes us further problems—sonic walls, for one."

Matt sighed. "Nothing is ever as we expect it will be. We even had a pass to get him out through the pod chute in Area 7." He produced the plastic chip that Calute had managed to acquire.

"Ah, well, that would have been useless anyway," informed Dorin. "Passes were changed yesterday. The new system involves something called an electronic bracelet, I think." He smiled as if proud of his ability to remember things he had no understanding of.

Varl patted him on his back. "Any idea how it works?"

Dorin shook his head. "But, I do know that if Braymar leaves Area 6 the bracelet will be activated automatically and cause him intense pain."

"Oh, great," moaned Matt. "Now we have two problems. Braymar isn't where we expected to find him, so all of Calute's information about the prisons and plans to get him out are useless, *and* he's wearing a security bracelet."

"Where's your optimism gone, Matt, my boy? The good news is that we can just about fit four of us in the submersible," said Varl.

"—If we can get the bracelet off," added Matt. "Any ideas how we can get it deactivated, Dorin?"

"I'm sure I can find out—but isn't there a more major problem to solve first?"

Varl nodded. "I guess I'd better start thinking about sonic walls."

* * * * *

"Dorin's been gone a long time," said Matt. "Do you think our plan will work?" He stared at Varl, looking for some evidence that their scheme was not altogether ludicrous.

Varl's eyes twinkled. "Well, at the moment we only have a basic idea. There are a lot of details that need to be thought through. But, I'd say that the odds are good—depending upon what Dorin is able to find out about vault codes, of course."

"I thought, being a scientist, that you didn't like working

with odds."

"I don't. I'd prefer something concrete, of course, my boy. But in this case, it's a risk, no matter how prepared we are. Besides, you keep reminding me that we are playing your game. So what are the odds of us winning?"

Now it was Matt who smiled. "Forget the odds—we *have* to win. I have to get home!"

The door swung open, and Dorin rushed in, carrying four sets of cushioned ear protectors. He thrust them into Varl's arms. "Told you I'd seen these in the pump house," he beamed. "The noise of the pumps and generators in there is deafening. It's no wonder the workers need these things."

"No one asked questions when you took them?" inquired Varl, examining them carefully.

Dorin shrugged. "Being in charge of one of the storerooms has its advantages. People just assume I'm replacing or restocking items."

"Well, these will do fine," said Varl, putting them in an empty space on one of the shelves. "Any luck with finding out about the vault codes?"

"It was hard to get the information without raising suspicion," Dorin answered, lowering himself carefully to the floor. "And if what I've heard is right, it's not going to be easy."

Matt and Varl sat next to him between two tall rows of shelving units.

Matt sighed. "Go on, let's have the worst of it. Keela will give up on us at this rate." He looked at his watch. "We've been here three hours already."

"The three controlling guards each has something called

a sonic encryptor, which transmits directly to the computer in the vault room from anywhere in Karn." Dorin crossed his legs. "When two of the three sonic encryptors have transmitted their codes, the vault program on the computer will open. The controlling guard on duty can then access the computer program to shut off the sonic wall in whichever sections he chooses."

Matt sighed. This time he felt as though the task was beyond them. "Wow! That's a tough one."

"Sonic encryptors, eh?" mumbled Varl.

"How can we ever get hold of *two* of them?" Matt thought out loud. He realized that his usual optimism was waning, and as an afterthought added, "There has to be a way."

"And there is," said Varl, scratching at his ever-growing beard. "A transmitter can be turned into a receiver quite easily. We need to get hold of just *one* encryptor before the vault is next opened. I can make some minor adjustments, pick up another code when one of the others transmits, and store it on the encryptor that we have. Our one encryptor will then transmit two codes."

Dorin nodded his approval. "Can't say I understand the scientific principles, but it seems a good enough idea."

"But, how long before the vault might be opened next?" asked Matt, not wanting to dampen their enthusiasm.

"Dorin?" Varl turned to his friend eagerly. "Any idea?"

"The vault is opened three times a day in order to remove or take out items; at eight, two and again at eight. There are regularly two guards, but six extra guards are present during the opening times."

Matt twisted his watchstrap around on his wrist to look at

the digital face. He smiled. "We missed the eight o'clock a.m. opening, of course, but we've still got just under two hours before the second opening."

"Um," said Varl. "That puts us over the four-hour limit that we discussed with Calute. The Area will be swarming with guards when the meeting ends."

"There are already patrols out there," Dorin informed. "I suspect the Senate session is already over."

"We've got to continue, now that we've come this far," begged Matt.

"Agreed," said Varl, patting Matt on the back. "If we can get hold of one of the off-duty guard's encryptors before 1:30, I can have it ready to receive the transmission before two. Think you can do it, Dorin?"

"Me?" said Dorin, stunned. He thought for a minute. "Zang it! I suppose it *has* to be me—you're both better off out of sight." He got to his feet, straightened his robe and paced between the rows of shelving looking at the different boxes. "Varl, can you reach one of these cardboard boxes on the top shelf?"

Varl walked to the end of the shelving and stared upward. He pulled out a small footstool, tucked underneath one of the units, and lifted down a large box that was surprisingly light.

"I'm intrigued," he said, handing it to Dorin. "What have you in mind?"

"Even several hundred Noxerans need bathroom tissue restocking," he said, winking. "It's a good excuse to get me into the guard accommodation in Area 8."

Matt laughed. "So this storeroom job does have its good

points, then?"

* * * * *

Dorin struggled off the pod chute, which linked Areas 6 and 8. He walked quietly along one of the bright corridors, the huge box blocking most of his vision, and turned into the common area at the end. Many off-duty legionaries were relaxing on the comfortable couches in the center. The room was filled with the sound of music and laughter.

"I heard that a boy said he was the nephew of the Princeps," recounted one elderly legionary.

Another clutched his sides and howled. "And Argus believed him?"

"Indeed! Then he told the Princeps what a pleasant young man his nephew was. Of course Balbus wanted to know, *what* nephew? It turns out he doesn't have one!"

The room erupted in raucous laughter.

A young legionary spoke up. "We all ought to be thankful Argus wasn't assigned vault guard duty. Where is he now?"

"Confined to his suite for his incompetence. He has been ordered on the next submarine back to Noxera!"

"What of the boy?" asked the same young man.

"Balbus has a search party looking for him *and* the boy's teacher. What's more," said the elderly legionary, "the Princeps' body guards are quietly looking for Senator Gallus, who offered to help them. It is unclear whether Gallus is a traitor or being held hostage!" The room erupted in frantic chatter once again.

Fear surged through Dorin's bones. He could hardly

place one foot in front of the other to continue his task. He perspired heavily as he made his way behind the group and into the living suites, keeping his face hidden behind the large box. His mind raced. How many Noxerans knew him as Senator Gallus and would be able to put his face to the name? Certainly one vault guard and several dozen legionaries. Time was running out. How long would it be before he was identified as an intruder and not a senator who had arrived from Noxera a few days before?

Dorin hastily began his search of the living suites. Several legionaries shared each suite. Most were empty, their occupants participating in the discussion in the common area. He had a vague idea what a sonic encryptor might look like—he thought he'd seen one in the vault room—but had no idea how he would get it from one of the guards.

Without success in the first twelve rooms, he entered the thirteenth suite already feeling depressed. It seemed an impossible task. He placed the box down by the bathroom door, as he had in every other suite. Feeling sick with nerves, he began to look through the drawers of clothes. The guards had few personal possessions. Only the occasional framed photo of a family member, a book, or a trinket was left lying about on the bureau or bedside table. Yet again his search was in vain. Dorin moved into the bathroom, put a token roll of toilet tissue in the cupboard and made a hasty retreat.

By the time that Dorin reached the twenty-seventh suite of rooms, he had wasted an hour and decided that the task was futile. There were only a few suites left to search. *A guard would probably keep such an important device on his person at all times*, he thought. The door to suite 827 was closed.

Dorin placed his identification chip up to the wall pad. The red light that flashed back at him indicated that the room was occupied and locked from the inside. He knocked loudly, hoping that the inhabitant of the room hadn't yet heard the news and didn't know him. The door slid open. A legionary, towel wrapped around his waist, stared down at Dorin.

"What do you want?" he asked bluntly.

Dorin's scanned the sour face. They had not met previously. He felt relieved, but still his hands shook slightly as he placed the box on the floor. "I'm here to restock your bathroom supplies."

The legionary groaned. "Can't you come back? I'm about to shower. I thought this was done at the beginning of the week."

Dorin shook his head, picked up the box and squeezed past into the room before any further objections could be made. He headed straight for the bathroom, glancing quickly around at cupboard surfaces on his way through. The legionary hovered momentarily in the bathroom doorway and then sat on the bed.

Dorin sighed heavily as he opened the bathroom cupboard and placed half a dozen rolls of toilet paper alongside the existing supply. He would be returning to Varl and Matt empty-handed.

His task complete, he picked up the box and turned toward the door. A silver object caught his attention by the washbasin. It was round, with a narrow gray screen, and was no larger than the palm of his hand. His heart quickened. Could this be what he was looking for? With trembling fingers he glanced over his shoulder.

The legionary got to his feet and started walking toward the bathroom. "Aren't you done yet?"

With his back to the open door, Dorin snatched the silver object off the surface, depositing it quickly in the box. He took a deep breath, and tried desperately to compose himself. Then he turned to face the legionary, who now leaned against the bathroom doorframe.

"You've . . . you've got enough for a month," Dorin stammered.

The guard raised his eyebrows and sniggered. "Then it didn't need restocking, did it?"

Finally, after what seemed a lifetime to Dorin, the guard moved to one side and allowed him to pass. Dorin walked quickly to the door. His heart slowed slightly as he stepped into the corridor and heard the door to suite 827 close firmly behind.

He walked the length of the corridor, his footsteps quickening as he reached the end. Would he make it back in time for Varl to change the sonic encryptor into a receiver? Had he actually *found* the sonic encryptor? There was no way he could stop and open the box to take a closer look at the object he had stolen.

He marched back through the common area, where the intense discussion continued between the off-duty legionaries, and around the corner in the direction of the pod chute. Several guards walked toward him. Dorin raised the box in front of his face as they passed. He descended the steps to the pod chute. The doors opened. Dorin placed the box in the cargo container and strapped himself into a seat for the journey back.

Two legionaries entered the pod just as the doors were closing. They sat down in the seats behind. Dorin tried to remain calm, but he could feel his pulse quicken and his hands become clammy. *Breathe deeply*, he told himself. After all, the legionaries would be looking at the back of his head for the short journey.

When the doors opened at the other end, Dorin hastily unclipped the metal fastener and rose from his seat. Without turning his head, he picked the box out of the cargo container and muttered, "Enjoy your day."

Dorin bolted down the gleaming corridor, up the stairs and across the open area, almost tripping over his feet. Panting heavily, he slipped quickly through the storeroom door and leaned against the nearest shelving unit to regain his breath. The room seemed strangely quiet. He looked around anxiously.

"Varl . . . Matt . . . where are you?" he gasped.

There was no response.

Chapter 12

Keela hauled herself out of the water and sat on the dock in the half-light. She twisted her long dark hair into a spiral to wring out the water and watched the moisture dry quickly off her golden skin. She was thankful that her genes allowed her to stay in the sea for so long without feeling cold. How could she begin to explain *what* she was to her new friends?

It had been several hours since Varl and Matt left to rescue Braymar, although it seemed much longer. By now Calute and Marcella would have returned from meeting with the Noxeran Senate. The promised hours of distraction were over—the legionaries would no longer be occupied in Area 7.

Keela knew that such a complicated task would take time, but a sinking feeling in the pit of her stomach told her that something had gone wrong. She clambered to her feet and hesitated before walking along the platform.

The tiny window was high up the watertight door. She found it difficult to raise herself up on the balls of her webbed feet. After several attempts to maintain her balance, she managed to stay poised long enough to stare through the little glass circle.

Keela gulped. The figure of a legionary loomed toward her. Panicked, she dived from the platform into the water, resurfacing close to the ladder to listen and wait. Would he pass by? She knew that Varl had succeeded in activating the red light above the door. Surely any legionary on patrol would not think to check the water level in the airlock?

Her heart sank as she focused on the two spotlights casting a low light on the platform. If only she had thought to turn them off! Even a faint glimmer through the small window would be enough to attract his attention. She clung to the metal rungs and waited . . . and waited—beginning to relax with every second that passed.

Then, her worst fears were realized. The huge sealing mechanism began to move, turning slowly clockwise. A loud metallic clunk preceded the groan of hinges as the heavy door opened. Keela looked at the submersible, barely visible in the blackness of the water. She pressed close to the ladder, listening as the footsteps clanked along the metal platform, and praying that the guard wouldn't see the outline of the small craft against the water.

The footsteps stopped abruptly directly above her. Keela heard the click of the legionary's communicator opening. She swallowed hard. This must mean that he had seen the vessel and was about to call in a report. Before long the airlock would be swarming with reinforcements, and Varl and Matt would not be able to return. She knew that she had to do something before the legionary told anyone.

In a moment of immense bravery, and before the legionary realized what was happening, Keela climbed up on the ladder and grabbed him by the ankle. With one enormous tug, she toppled him off balance and pulled him over the edge of the dock. He yelled as he hit the water with a loud smack. The communicator flew from his hands and disappeared below the surface.

Keela, startled by her own courage, wondered what she could do next to prevent him from fetching help. Within minutes he would be out of the water and running for the door. Her eyes fell on a coil of rope, which hung on a metal spike on the wall above the platform. It was fairly thick—probably used to moor the submersibles—but it would do.

A faint voice in the water shook her out of her thoughts. She turned to see the legionary struggling to stay above the surface.

"Help me, please!" he begged. "I'm drown . . ." His arms began to flail. He thrashed around madly.

Keela stared in horror as the legionary swallowed water, gulping and spluttering, splashing and kicking.

"Help me!" he managed to utter again.

Then it was quiet. He disappeared into the darkness, slipping silently away. Ripples on the surface showed the only trace of his struggle.

"What am I doing?" shouted Keela to herself, facing the reality of what had just happened. She leaped off the steps and plunged below the surface to find him. Frantically, in the darkness of the water, she swam about searching for the man who had been unable to swim to the side. *Or had the weight of his lorica pulled him under? No matter which*, she thought, *he cannot die by my hands.*

Something knocked against her body as she felt along the murky bottom. With relief at her good fortune, Keela grabbed the legionary under his armpits and, using all her power, heaved him upward. Again she was thankful for her genes. Her aquatic build gave her powerful upper body muscles. Even so, the legionary's weight almost kept her from surfacing. Determined to save his life, she found the extra strength she needed to bring his head above water.

Breathing heavily, she grabbed for the ladder with her left hand while still supporting the legionary with her other hand. She clung tightly to the rungs, wondering how she would get him onto the platform.

"One step at a time," she said to herself. "I will do it one step at a time."

By lunging for the next rung and pushing forcefully up with her feet, she inched her way up the ladder. After several precarious moments, when she felt sure she could hold his weight no longer, she took hold of the upper rung. By wedging herself between the handrails she managed to heave his upper body onto the platform. His legs dangled over the edge, his body lifeless.

Keela clambered onto the platform. Puffing and panting, she dragged the legionary away from the edge. Quickly she rolled him over onto his back and began pumping furiously on his chest.

"Please, do not die," she begged. "I did not want you to die . . . just wanted to stop you . . ."

He remained lifeless. She pumped on his chest again and slapped his face.

"I will not let you—do you hear?"

The legionary spluttered and coughed up water. His eyes fluttered. Keela stood over him and drew in breath. She had succeeded. He was alive. She congratulated herself on a job well done.

The legionary was regaining his senses. The black vidium hanging from his belt caught her attention. What was she thinking? This was the enemy!

Keela knew that the vidium might not work after being immersed in seawater, but she could not take the risk and she had no idea how to use it. She whipped it from the holster and threw it into the water.

As the legionary began to move his arms, horror swept over her again. Even without a weapon, he was still a threat. Keela lunged for the rope hanging on the wall. The guard's eyes met hers as she tied it frantically around his wrists.

He began to struggle. Keela fought against his thrashing legs. She brought the rope from his wrists down to his ankles. Lifting his feet, she wrapped it roughly up his legs and over his chest to his head, coiling it around his neck. She finished by tightly tying the two ends together. The legionary glared at her. Thank goodness his fight for survival in the water had drained his energy, and he had been no match for her speed and strength.

He coughed up more water and found his voice. "Help . . . someone help," he called in a feeble manner.

Keela glanced along the platform. The door was still open! Someone might hear! She lifted the bottom of her tunic to her mouth. Gritting her teeth over the fabric she tore the edge of her garment and ripped off a strip. She stuffed it into the legionary's mouth and sprinted the distance to the door. Keela pushed it closed, relieved that no other guard had ventured their way during the last dramatic minutes.

Exhausted, she turned off the lights and slumped in the darkness at the feet of her prisoner.

"Varl, Matt, please come back soon," she whispered.

* * * * *

The rectangular air vent in the ceiling of the storeroom moved slightly.

"Hey, Dorin, we're in here," whispered Matt, pushing down on the grid. "Stand back, in case it falls."

A fine layer of plaster sprinkled downward, lightly icing Dorin's hair. Dorin looked up just as the vent came crashing down. He extended his arms as a natural reflex and caught the plastic cover before it hit the floor.

Matt's bare legs dangled in midair searching for a resting place. Finally he found his footing and lowered himself precariously onto the top of the shelving.

"Great catch," he complimented, looking down at Dorin. He studied the old man's bewildered expression. "We had you worried, eh?"

Dorin nodded. "Just a little."

"Sorry. We had a minor emergency while you were gone."

Matt helped Varl locate the top shelf before beginning the climb down. He jumped the last three feet and grinned at Dorin. "I don't really like heights, but *up* is always a good way out of trouble."

Varl lowered himself to the floor in a less-than-agile manner. "My bones are too old for these kind of antics," he grumbled.

"What happened?" Dorin asked, when they both stood in front of him.

"We heard a commotion in the corridor," said Varl breathlessly. "Just as well we decided to play it safe, because a patrol of legionaries searched the storeroom minutes after we'd found the hiding place."

"I was worried you might have visitors," replied Dorin.

"We were worried you'd been caught!" Matt retorted.

Dorin smiled. "Thanks for your concern. Is this what you wanted?" He felt along the bottom of the box, under the remaining rolls of bathroom tissue, and produced the small silver object.

"Could be," Varl answered, examining it carefully. "It'll take me a few minutes to tell."

"A few minutes is all you've got," said Matt, looking at his watch. "There's only twenty-five minutes before the other sonic encryptors transmit to open the vault."

Varl opened up his leather satchel and pulled out a selection of tiny tools. He placed them on the ground and arranged them in order. "If this *is* an encryptor it will take less time than that," he said, confidently unclipping the back.

Matt and Dorin leaned over Varl, anxiously watching him work.

"Well?" Dorin asked. "Did I get the right thing?"

Varl didn't reply. His fingers were surprisingly nimble. Occasionally he grunted or groaned. Matt kept looking at his watch, watching every second tick by. He knew that the next few minutes were vital if they were to free Braymar and get back to the submersible before it was discovered.

"Ten minutes left," he felt compelled to announce.

Varl grunted again and continued as before. Dorin stood upright and rubbed his back. His face was creased with worry.

"Zang it! Five minutes left," said Matt, panicked. "You've got to hurry." He felt sick inside. Time was definitely running out, and Varl had said nothing for twenty minutes. He looked at Dorin, who chewed on his bottom lip. Dorin shrugged when he caught Matt's eyes.

With two minutes to go, Matt felt the need to cross his fingers behind his back. *A dumb thing to do*, he told himself, *but it can't hurt*. He stared at Varl's face trying to read his expression for some sign of success, but the elderly scientist gave nothing away.

"Bingo!" said Varl finally. A broad grin spread across his cheeks.

Matt sighed. "That's what I call cutting it close!"

Varl winked at him. "What do you mean? I had one minute to spare!" He switched on the sonic encryptor. A small green light flickered on the edge of the device.

They waited—all three pairs of eyes focused on the gray rectangle, watching eagerly for something to happen. The minutes ticked by.

Matt looked at his watch again. Two o'clock passed by. He imagined sections of the sonic wall deactivating. Perhaps if he wished for it to happen, it would. After another two minutes elapsed with still no success, he felt obliged to tell the others. "I make it 2:04," he said, swallowing hard.

Varl smacked the encryptor in the palm of his hand.

"Do you think you did something wrong?" asked Dorin.

Varl pursed his lips and didn't reply.

"2:06," said Matt quietly. He had almost given up hope. Varl would have to work on the encryptor some more. They would have to try again at eight o'clock.

Varl's shoulders slumped. He smiled, let out a deep breath, and beckoned Matt to look. "It's working! The guards must have transmitted late."

Small black numbers churned across the screen. Finally they slowed, and the screen went blank.

"Zang it!" mumbled Dorin. "Now what's happened?"

Matt could not hide his disappointment. "I guess it failed."

"Why do you say that?" asked Varl, who showed no signs of frustration.

"Where's the code? Shouldn't it be displayed on the screen?"

Varl put his arm around Matt's shoulders. "Doubtful, I'd say. The code is stored where it's needed—in the memory. If it were displayed on the screen, anyone could copy it down and key it into another transmitting device later."

"So, we just have to trust that this encryptor will now hold both codes?" asked Dorin. His face crumpled.

"That about sums it up. We won't know if it worked 'til we try," said Varl. "I suggest we wait thirty minutes to allow the extra vault guard time to depart, and then get on with the next part of our plan. Besides, I need time to change the encryptor back from a receiver to a transmitter."

Matt was concerned. "If we leave it too long the guard will realize his encryptor is missing, and the entire Noxeran army will descend upon the vault room."

"The vault guard may have already discovered his encryptor is missing," said Dorin, contorting his face into a gloomy expression.

Varl gave him a sideways glance. "True. We'll just have

to hope we time it right. I don't think three of us can tackle eight guards."

"Agreed," said Dorin, beginning to collect things they would need from various boxes on the shelves.

Matt grabbed the four sets of ear protectors and handed them to Dorin in silence. Still deep in his own thoughts, he carefully lifted his computer from its hiding place and gave it to Varl to put in his satchel. Once again, he was putting his faith in Varl's technological wizardry. But this time Matt had severe doubts. Would they succeed in freeing Braymar and be able to move onto the next part of his game? Or was their whole crazy plan doomed to fail from the start?

Chapter 13

Varl pressed his ear to the storeroom door. It was quiet outside.

"Okay," he said, heaving the bulging satchel over his shoulder. "We'll take the chance and go."

They crept down the stairs and paused at the bottom. Varl peered around the corner. He ducked back again. Already they had encountered problems. Two legionaries were talking outside the vault room. Varl put his finger to his lips and motioned the others to stay back out of sight.

After several minutes they heard footsteps. The legionaries were walking toward them. Varl moved back a step and pressed close to the wall, praying that the guards wouldn't take the stairs. He clenched the stunner tightly in his right hand and held his breath as the footsteps grew nearer. The chattering continued but the legionaries passed by the entrance.

Varl motioned to Matt and Dorin. With trepidation they approached the vault room.

"Know what to do?" Varl whispered.

They nodded. Dorin raised his identification chip to the pad and the huge doors slid smoothly open. He held himself in a dignified manner and proceeded resolutely down the narrow walkway toward the guard cubicle. Varl immediately activated the sonic encryptor and followed Dorin down the walkway, Matt close on his heels.

Carella appeared, stretching and yawning. His relaxed expression changed and his mannerisms turned hostile the instant he laid eyes on Dorin. He gripped his vidium.

"Carella, I'm glad that you are still here," said Dorin in a friendly, jovial tone.

"I wish I could say the same," he retorted. "It's nearing the end of a very long shift, and now your appearance will make it even longer."

The other guard appeared from behind the cubicle and joined Carella on the walkway. He eyed them with suspicion and made sure that his weapon was visible.

Dorin laughed. "And why should that be?"

"Because this entire realm has been looking for you and these strangers for the past two hours. Did you not realize, Senator Gallus?"

"Certainly not. I've been doing my job and trying to locate one of the centurions for permission to open the vault as you instructed." Dorin waved the cushioned ear protectors in front of Carella, as if they were part of his storeroom activities. "I suggest you report our arrival here to your superior so that we can get this mess cleared up immediately."

Carella's eyes widened, seemingly taken aback by this request. Dorin pushed past him into the guard cubicle. Carella and the other guard quickly followed him in, leaving Varl and Matt hovering in the doorway.

Dorin continued to distract Carella and the guard, with talk of permission letters and vault codes. Varl winked at Matt and moved between Carella and the computer, allowing

Matt to inch closer and closer toward the keyboard.

Shielded by Varl's large frame, Matt turned and began accessing the program. Varl hoped that the boy would be able to pull up the controls for the sonic wall. Trapped air was vibrated at a set frequency. Matt would have to change the frequency settings to 15,000Hz as he had been instructed. At this frequency the wall would become ineffective, but the sound given off would be deafening to the human ear. Varl imagined Matt flashing through the menu screens trying to find the correct one.

"Where's the boy?" shouted Carella. "Who's using the keyboard?" He pushed past Dorin, drew his vidium and shoved Varl to one side.

"Get away from there!" he bellowed at Matt, sticking the vidium into the boy's back.

Varl whipped the stunner from his pocket and thrust it against Carella's neck. Carella's knees buckled and he fell to the floor. The other guard immediately pulled his vidium from its holster and took aim. Without pausing for thought, Varl stepped in front of Matt, quite prepared to die for the boy.

Varl held his breath, fearing the worst. But instead of firing, the legionary dropped his weapon and threw his hands over his ears. He began yelling and contorting his body in agony. Varl gritted his teeth in an attempt to block out the pain. Matt had finished entering the required computer sequence just in time.

Dorin fought to put on ear protectors and threw a set to Varl and Matt, who were struggling to maintain their composure with the piercing sound.

Varl opened his satchel and produced a large roll of plastic tape that Dorin had borrowed from the storeroom. He kicked the vidium out of reach and bound the guard's ankles. As Varl began winding the tape around his wrists, the guard frantically struggled to keep his fingertips over his ears.

"Okay, let's get Braymar. Matt, find the key to the electronic bracelet," shouted Varl, adjusting the cushioning over his ears. He realized that neither of his friends had heard his instructions, but they knew the plan and looked like they were setting about their tasks.

Dorin barged past. Varl followed him to Braymar. The Freedom Fighter was curled in a ball on the ground, trying to protect his ears from the shrill sound.

They hauled Braymar to his feet, thrust ear protectors over his wild black hair, and ushered him down the walkway toward the door. Braymar complied happily, although Varl realized from his dazed expressions that he had no idea whether they were his enemy or his rescuers.

Matt was nowhere to be seen. Varl motioned to Dorin and Braymar to wait by the door. He tore back down the walkway and into the guard cubicle where the boy was furiously searching for the key.

Matt shook his head. "I've looked in every possible place, but can't find it," he shouted.

Varl understood even though he couldn't hear the words. He turned in circles, racking his brain as to where a guard would keep the key to a prisoner's bracelet. Time was running out. He had no idea if an alarm registered elsewhere in Karn when the sonic wall was deactivated. For all he knew, more legionaries were already on their way.

He looked at the motionless body of Carella, still unconscious on the floor. *Of course,* he thought, *the guard would keep it with him.* Varl knelt down on the floor and felt for pockets in Carella's lorica. There were none. But around his neck a thin silver chain caught Varl's eye. Varl tugged it free from under the tunic top. Hanging on the end was a flat electronic key, the size of Varl's thumbnail. He yanked it from the chain, grabbed Matt by the elbow, and whipped him out of the cubicle.

"Okay, let's go!" he shouted to Dorin, gesturing to him to open the doors.

Once they were back in the corridor, the deafening sound was barely audible. Varl removed his ear protectors and told the others to do the same as they ran toward the airlock.

"Braymar, you will experience severe pain as we exit Area 6. We'll remove the bracelet when we're all safely in the airlock," he said, panting. "We can't stop now."

They reached the watertight door. "We've done it!" said Varl. The light still shone red above. Varl began to turn the mechanism. The lock clicked once, then twice. Dorin helped him heave open the door.

"Halt, or we fire," a loud voice warned.

Varl shuddered—he had spoken too soon. Reinforcements had arrived. He stopped and turned, raising his hands slowly in the air. The others did the same. A row of armed legionaries blocked the corridor. His mind searched for a way out. He knew that only one or two of them might get through the open door safely if the legionaries opened fire. Calute had warned him about the vidium. With its double laser, it could strike down two opponents at once.

If he and Dorin took the brunt of the force, would Matt and Braymar make it to the submersible? It seemed an impossible situation. It would take at least ten minutes for the chamber to flood and for Keela to open the airlock—not quick enough to stop the guards from attacking the sub itself. He stared at the row of weapons aimed at them. There seemed to be no way out.

As if someone heard his thoughts, the ground began to rumble and the corridor shook, lightly at first. Matt fell backward through the open door and Braymar stumbled after him. Dorin fell to the ground, only a few feet from the escape route. With weapons hindering their balance, the guards grabbed for the walls. But, in attempting to aim their vidiums and stay standing, they only succeeded in tripping over each other.

The rumbling intensified. Varl could no longer stay on his feet. He managed to crawl through the exit after the others, slamming his side against the metal edge as another tremor took hold. He reached for Dorin's long gown and tried to pull his friend through.

Varl could hear the shouts of the guards and then the random firing of the weapons. Dorin screamed in pain. He had been hit in the leg. Matt held on to the steel edge of the doorframe for support. He grabbed Dorin's wrist and helped Varl drag him through the door. Together they fought the tremors and closed the airlock as more weapons were fired.

Varl forced one of his tools behind the locking mechanism to stop it from turning. He knew that it wouldn't prevent the legionaries from breaking through eventually, but it might give him and his friends the extra minutes needed to get the submersible out to sea.

Keela turned on the spotlights and staggered toward them. "You made it back," she said, sighing deeply.

"Keela, help me get Dorin to the sub!" shouted Varl. "Matt, here's the electronic key—help Braymar!"

Braymar was battling forward on his hands and knees. From the look on his face, Varl guessed he was trying to ignore the intense pain caused by the activation of the electronic bracelet. Matt took the key from Varl and scrambled toward Braymar. He searched for the slot in the side of the bracelet. The key slipped into position and, as if by magic, the bracelet fell apart. Braymar rubbed his wrists vigorously and then turned back to help Varl.

Dorin's leg was badly burned from the vidium blast, and he had blacked out. The platform shook and flexed with the continuing tremors, but Varl was determined to get him to the submersible. He was not about to leave his good friend to die at the hands of the Noxerans. Progress was slow. Every foot they dragged him took a great deal of effort.

As they neared the submersible, Varl noticed the tied-up guard. He raised his eyebrows, realizing that Keela had had problems while they were gone. If they left the legionary where he was, the guard would drown as the airlock flooded.

"He'll have to come with us," shouted Varl. "I'll not be responsible for the death of any man, and we can't leave him here."

"But he *can't* come," replied Matt. "There's no room in the submersible—four people maximum, remember? There are now five of us."

"Wrong," said Braymar, removing his shoes. "There are four of you." He proudly displayed his webbed feet. "I can go with Keela."

The tremors subsided, but there was no time to debate with the guards close behind.

"That settles it. The legionary *is* coming," Varl said emphatically. "Matt, we'll need you at the bottom end of the ladder. Take the stunner and watch the guard."

Matt ran nimbly along the narrow top of the submersible and opened the hatch in preparation. He climbed inside.

Varl cut the legionary's rope. "Get in and stay quiet or you'll be left here to drown!" he ordered.

The legionary paused for a second and looked Varl in the eye. Varl knew that he was weighing up his chances of escape as none of them were armed. Without hesitation Varl pulled a heavy wrench from his satchel and waved it in the air.

"Don't think I won't throw this at you," shouted Varl.

Braymar moved next to Varl, his tall, muscular frame dwarfing the young man. "Get inside now!" Braymar bellowed, lunging forward.

The legionary turned and walked slowly along the submersible toward the hatch.

"Quickly," Varl spat, realizing that the he was deliberately stalling for time. He watched the guard climb down the ladder and breathed deeply.

"You had better hurry. The Noxerans are attempting to open the airlock door," said Braymar. "Keela is starting the flooding process."

"Good luck, Braymar. We'll see you both in Area 1," said

Varl, stepping over the edge of the hatch.

"Do not worry about us. We will open the outer doors as soon as we can," he replied.

Braymar picked up Dorin. He lowered him down to Varl, who laid the old man onto the only available floor space and then quickly closed the hatch.

Matt was standing over the legionary with the stunner aimed at his neck. Varl opened his satchel and took out the roll of tape. Space was very tight with two extra people on board. With his legs straddled over Dorin's unconscious body, he bound the guard's wrists and then taped him around his waist to the swivel chair. Satisfied that the legionary could cause no trouble, he squeezed into his seat at the console and turned on the power.

"Okay, Matt, my boy, program the coordinates."

"I can hear the doors opening."

"Good. Let's get this heap of ancient technology out of here and get Dorin back to Area 1 for treatment."

Matt muttered something inaudible as they escaped into the open sea. Varl chuckled, realizing that what he termed a heap of ancient technology was a futuristic vessel to the boy.

* * * * *

The room was painted a clinical white and contained little furniture. It was a stark contrast to the warm colors and soft furnishings found everywhere else in Karn. Matt stared at Dorin's body lying on one of the six beds in the Area 2 medical center. He cared deeply about the old man.

Covered in a white sheet, pale and motionless, Dorin looked as though he would never move again. Targon and Varl stood opposite in silence.

Keela came up from behind and gently put her hand on Targon's shoulder. "He will be fine, I promise," she said quietly. "It was a severe shock to his system, but Doc says he will make a full recovery with plenty of rest."

The door opened. Calute marched in triumphantly, followed closely by Marcella. They both wore bright, multi-colored tunics, adorned with lavish jewelry. Their bright attire and jubilant mood annoyed Matt.

Targon sniffed back the tears. "What about his leg?"

"He was very lucky. He will not lose it, if that is what you are asking. But it will always be scarred," replied Keela.

"Dorin was not the only lucky one," Calute added. "Had it not been for the earthquake, none of you would have lived to tell the tale."

Varl moved away from the bedside. He walked over to Marcella and Calute and in an adamant tone replied, "I'm sure that's true, but we *are* here to tell the tale. Not only that, we rescued Braymar. We've proved our loyalty to Karn. Tell us everything about the Noxerans."

"I think it's time you were honest with us," said Matt, feeling angry.

Calute glanced at Marcella before responding. "Indeed it is. We are forever grateful for your bravery in returning Braymar, but for us the battle is just beginning."

Marcella stepped forward and took Varl's hand. "I knew when you arrived in Karn that your presence here was not by chance. You were *meant* to come and assist us in our hour of need. Please allow us a moment of celebration before we must again face our troubles. If you would care to freshen up in your suite and then join us in the nourishment center, we have our own way to say thank you. And yes—your questions will be answered."

* * * * *

Nonius Balbus paced the Senate floor, anger clearly visible in his bulging eyes. His face twitched uncontrollably as Tacitus recounted the events leading up to the escape of Braymar.

"Incompetent fools!" Balbus roared. "How did a patrol of my legionaries allow an unarmed group of old men and children to outwit them?"

"I am sure the earth tremors played a major part in their success, Princeps," Tacitus suggested. He bit his lip in anticipation of the reply.

Balbus banged his hand down on the central table. He flexed his fingers and then clenched his hand tightly into a fist until his thumb and forefinger turned white. He turned slowly to face Tacitus, flicking his head in an apparent attempt to stop the annoying twitch.

"Earth tremors? There's always some excuse! The old man and the boy pose as my nephew and his guardian—and no one thinks to confirm this with me immediately? Patrols can't locate them for the next two hours, and *then* they manage to deactivate the sonic wall and take Braymar and a guard from under our noses!" His voice rose to screaming pitch. "What kind of second-rate army have I got here?

Caesar would turn in his grave!"

Tacitus flinched and closed his mouth. In this mood, the Princeps was capable of anything. Tacitus decided that it would be better not to respond. He did not want to be the next to suffer his leader's wrath.

Balbus cleared his throat. "The guards who allowed this to happen will be held accountable. I hope they have been confined to quarters."

"Of course, Princeps."

"Can the legionary who was taken hostage be trusted to hold his tongue?"

"I believe he is a loyal and trustworthy follower." Tacitus paused, aware that he didn't sound convincing, and added, "He will not betray you."

"Mmm," said Balbus, mulling over the response. He folded his flabby arms across his belly. "I cannot take the risk that he might talk. Call an immediate meeting of the Senate."

"Are you sending legionaries to take Braymar and the guard back by force?" asked Tacitus.

"No. It is time to move forward with our plan. We've wasted enough months striving for accuracy—we're near enough with our calculations. I can't afford any more mishaps to interfere with our long-term goal."

"Would it still not be wise to rescue the guard?"

"Do not question my decisions, or I might just leave you here to die with the Karns!" Balbus spat. He raised his bushy eyebrows and glared at Tacitus.

"I apologize, Princeps. I assumed you would seek retribution."

"The Karns have found courage of late, and will almost

certainly offer resistance. I cannot afford to have a battle on my hands with so few men. Every legionary will be needed in Noxera when we build the new empire."

"Understood, Princeps."

Balbus narrowed his eyes and snorted, "The people of Karn will pay dearly for crossing me yet again."

Chapter 14

Matt looked up as Varl sauntered into the living area of their suite. Targon drummed his fingers against the edge of the glass of water he was holding.

"I'd forgotten how good it felt to have a clean-shaven face," Varl said, rubbing his chin.

"Actually, I thought you looked distinguished with a beard, *Senator*," said Matt, with a grin. He smoothed his hands over his tunic. "I must admit, these things don't seem so bad when you've had to wear a lorica for a few hours."

"I'm just glad that Dorin's okay," mumbled Targon.

Varl nodded. "Agreed. It's not easy for someone of Dorin's age to recover from such a shock to the system. I'm relieved he's going to make a full recovery."

"And so am I," said Matt. "But now we've got Braymar safely back, we'd better find out the next step in my game." He sat cross-legged on the floor and opened up his laptop.

Targon leaped off his chair, almost spilling the glass of water in his hand. He glared down at Matt. "Are you totally insensitive? You're not seriously going to continue with your computer game after what just happened, are you?"

Matt stopped typing and looked up, surprised by his objection. "You didn't complain in Zaul," he replied.

"That's because my life was over if things stayed the way

they were. No one in Zaul had anything to lose by following you and your game rules. We are safe and comfortable with the people of Karn. I don't think we should risk more injury or death to any of us!"

Matt felt both anger and sadness. While he understood Targon's reluctance to continue, he resented his friend's attitude.

"And what about me? Doesn't *my* life, and what I have left behind, count for anything?" He tried to contain his emotions and speak calmly, but he heard his voice rise anyway. "I *miss* my home. I *want* to get home, Targon. And playing the game is the only way I know how. None of us belong here."

Varl placed his hand firmly on Targon's shoulder. "It's not as simple as either of you would like to believe. The Karns fear death by the Noxerans, the earthquakes get worse every day, and our rescue of Braymar may have dire consequences for all of us. Balbus will be so outraged, there's no telling what he might do in retaliation. In fact, I'm surprised the legionaries haven't already stormed and taken hostages."

Targon looked frightened. "You think we're at risk, too?"

"Almost certainly," said Varl. "You will not feel this safety and comfort much longer. Then what reason will you have to stay in Karn?"

Targon lowered his head and muttered, "Then I hope we *can* get back to Zaul."

"Also, it seems that Marcella believes we were sent here by some power or other to help them," added Varl.

Matt gasped. "And you let her believe that?"

Varl shrugged. "I didn't say otherwise, because we need them as much as they *believe* they need us. Don't you see? We all want the same thing. We need to free the people of Karn and destroy the Keeper to win your game and get out of here, and they want their freedom from the Noxerans."

"But we're hardly their guardian angels—or whatever it is she thinks we are," said Matt.

Varl gave Matt a wry smile. "Do *you* want to try and explain to them that they are only characters in Level 2 of your computer game?"

"Point taken," said Matt, feeling glum. He stared at the blank computer screen in quiet contemplation.

Varl patted him on the back and lowered himself carefully to the floor. "So what are you waiting for? Let's get on with it. We need to establish who the Keeper is. Pull up the next riddle, my boy."

Targon sighed and kneeled down on the carpet. "Nonius Balbus—it has to be," he offered, peering over Varl's shoulder.

The familiar beauty of the ocean life around Karn dominated the computer screen in vivid colors. The repetitive fanfare of music followed the eerie voice, which announced, "Entering Level 2; Keeper of the Realm. Those who enter may never return."

Targon cowered noticeably. He changed his sitting position several times before settling down to listen.

Matt pulled up the menu and clicked on *'Rules'* once again. He scrolled down until he found number 9, *'The Keeper'.*

He turned to Varl and then looked thoughtfully at Targon.

"Okay, are you ready to listen to the rhyme?"

They nodded. The picture on the screen dramatically changed from the delightful beauty of the underwater environment to a room filled with machinery, accompanied by deafening noise.

"*Where* is that?" asked Targon, covering his ears and moving back from the screen.

"The pump house," said Varl instantly.

"How do you know?" asked Matt.

"I recognize the sound of pumps and generators—noisy things. If Dorin were here, I'm sure he'd confirm it. He took the ear protectors from the pump house, so he's been there."

"What relevance do you think this has to the Keeper?" said Matt, moving the cursor to click on the riddle.

Varl shrugged. "I really would hate to guess."

A computerized voice interrupted the conversation. In a stilted soprano tone the rhyme was read.

What at first seems an innocent plan
May cause the fall of modern man.
Let not a new dictator rise
The Keeper is the means of his demise.
Below the sea your answer falls
Beyond the Realm of Karn's watery walls
Destroying the Keeper, simple it seems
Will hurt those you love and end your dreams.

The picture instantly faded and the word '*Menu*' was left flashing on an otherwise blank screen.

"Whew!" said Matt, resting his back against a comfy

chair. "It doesn't tell us much, does it?"

"No question, the rhyme is more difficult to solve this time," agreed Varl. "There's not much in the way of clues as to who the Keeper is."

Matt walked across the room and poured himself a glass of water. He turned to look at the others. "I don't think we were right when we guessed Nonius Balbus."

Targon's face seemed to brighten. "Why do you say that?"

"Because Balbus is the only dictator around here and the rhyme says the Keeper is the *means* of his demise," Matt explained.

"I have to agree," said Varl, getting to his feet and rubbing his knees. "What's the time, Matt, my boy?"

"Only 6 p.m.," sighed Matt. "We've done so much today, it feels like midnight."

"I could do with some sleep, too. But we promised we'd meet Marcella and Calute in the nourishment center."

"More pills and pink liquid!" Targon groaned.

"Just smile and be grateful," said Matt, closing the computer and putting it carefully on the table. He opened the door with his identification chip and stood back for Varl. "Are you going to push them for information?"

"Very carefully. I'm sure there's a whole lot more to this than we understand, and they promised me some answers tonight. Let's see what information they offer and how it links with the riddle. Oh, and Matt . . . let's not mention your computer game—it might confuse the issue."

Targon laughed. "That's an understatement!"

* * * * *

Varl stared at the table. His eyes widened when he realized that pink liquid and pills would not be on the menu for dinner. Marcella had placed an enormous banquet table in front of the nourishment hatches and decorated it with an elaborate white cloth and garish red centerpiece. On numerous plates, staggered around the edge, were placed a variety of seaweed, fish, and seafood dishes that made his mouth water.

"Wow!" said Targon in a breathless voice.

Matt walked the length of the table in awe. "Thank you, Marcella. You've gone to a lot of trouble."

"It pleases you?" Keela asked.

"You bet!" said Targon, stretching out his hand to take one of the delicacies. His fingers were within inches of the plate when Varl managed to catch his attention.

"Manners," mouthed Varl.

Targon withdrew his hand quickly.

Marcella smiled. "I am so glad that you all approve. Please go ahead and eat. I hope that you will take as much as you want."

Braymar rushed forward to greet Varl. He held out his hand and shook Varl's firmly. "I cannot begin to tell you how grateful I am," he said in a genuine voice. "I am not only indebted that you saved my life, but in rescuing me, you have enabled us to continue with our plan."

"I'm pleased that it worked out for all of us," replied Varl, taking an empty plate from the stack. He walked the length of the banquet table and piled his plate high. Calute ushered him to the side of the room where chairs had been arranged in a group.

Varl began to munch on the enormous shrimp. "Aren't you joining us?" he asked with a full mouth.

Calute smiled. "Our stomachs were not built for such things."

Varl swallowed and looked him in the eye. "I'd be pleased if you would be honest about your background. I'm intrigued. You're obviously not human, but neither do you appear to be androids."

"Correctly deduced. We are Pisceans," said Braymar proudly.

Varl interrupted excitedly, his suspicions confirmed. "So named after the zodiac sign of the fish—*Pisces*. I assume that you'll now tell me you are half man and half fish!"

"Not quite," said Calute, seemingly taken aback by Varl's abruptness. "We are genetically altered humans, created by Dr. Willard Karn, and suitably engineered for life on the ocean floor."

Varl was about to bite into a large shrimp. He paused in midair and then set it down. His scientific curiosity had been aroused. Food was no longer his main thought. "Really? I'm impressed! I often wondered if genetic engineering to such a degree would be possible."

Calute continued with his explanation. "Originally from Noxera, Dr. Karn recognized the limitations of humans studying sea-life at this depth. He was particularly interested in underwater currents, and the fault lines, which are numerous in this area. When this research center was constructed, Willard Karn knew that decompression chambers would have to be used every time that a diver came back from an exploration exercise." He paused for breath.

Varl was so intrigued he sat with his mouth open.

Calute continued. "While robotic technology was available for much of the gathering of species and information, Dr. Karn knew that human hands and eyes were infinitely better to gather knowledge first hand. His greatest dream was to create a human fish—a human with the ability to stay for long periods underwater without requiring oxygen."

"And so you were successfully genetically engineered," summarized Varl.

Calute shook his head. "Not quite. Willard Karn died thinking that his experimentation had failed. His first test-tube prodigies showed the necessary characteristics but acted as humans. Their gills did not function and their skin could not cope with staying underwater unprotected for any length of time. When Willard Karn died, and the Noxerans decided the research center was outdated, the Pisceans were left to survive on their own."

"So, how did you come to be as you are?" asked Varl, who still hadn't touched another bite of food in his excitement.

"We are fifth and sixth generation Pisceans. By some incredible natural mutation that has taken place over the last one hundred and fifty years, we now have the ability to use either our lungs or our gills. We can breathe on land and also stay underwater for long periods of time." He pointed to the fine red marks on his neck.

"I had wondered about those," said Varl, leaning forward

to observe the fine slits more closely.

Braymar interrupted. "As I showed you in the airlock, our feet have developed to allow better movement in the water and our skin has grown an outer protective covering."

"Your gold-colored skin—amazing!" said Varl. "It's all utterly amazing! Is that why the Noxerans are here? Are they attempting to use you for their own needs or research in some way?"

Braymar laughed. "Indeed, no. The Noxerans have no knowledge that Willard Karn actually succeeded. We have kept this quiet for years, knowing that we would become a tourist attraction or declared 'freaks of nature' if the truth ever got out. You are the first to be trusted with our secret."

Varl bowed his head. "I'm honored . . . and your secret is safe with me." He put his plate on a side table. Food was no longer of interest with a technological revelation such as this. "So why *are* the Noxerans here?"

Calute answered. "Braymar has uncovered a plot by Nonius Balbus to take over Noxera, a coastal principality fifty miles to the north of us. Nonius Balbus does not approve of the current Noxeran government."

Braymar brushed back his wild hair from his eyes and continued the story. "We suspect that not only does he intend to do away with the existing Noxeran Senate, but that once he is in power he will do away with *his* mock senate in Karn and become a dictator."

"He is already a dictator," said Marcella. "No legionary dares cross him. I doubt if any senator would go against his wishes for fear of what he might do. Balbus has grandiose ideas of becoming the next Caesar." She pulled up a chair and joined the gathering.

Varl finally gave in once again to his hunger. He picked up his plate and bit into some pink salmon. "How do you suppose Balbus intends to do this? One would assume he'd gather an army and march on Noxera."

Braymar pursed his lips and shook his head. "Balbus has a very small following of around five hundred. Three hundred live here and are rotated with the two hundred living quietly on the mainland. Noxera is a huge principality with a well-organized army and loyal people. There is no other support for Balbus and no way that he would succeed with conventional methods."

"What *do* you know for certain?" asked Varl.

"We know that he expanded the drilling along the fault line when he arrived, and installed more pumps and generators to harness more electricity," replied Braymar. "What he is doing with that electricity, or how it will help him overrun Noxera, we are not sure."

"Hmm," said Varl, enjoying the seafood. "I'll think on this—see what I can come up with."

"I know the guard rotations and have accurate diagrams of the pumping and generating equipment," said Braymar proudly.

"Good," said Varl. "That could help me. I'd like to see those plans."

"There is one pressing problem," said Marcella, sadness in her voice. "I am sorry to change the tone of this celebratory party, but we promised to tell you the full situation. Balbus has demanded that we deliver six Karns as his slaves, by first light tomorrow, in compensation for

Braymar's meddling."

Calute sighed. "We have posted twenty able-bodied men, armed with our very limited weapons, by the pod chute to Area 7."

"Good," said Varl. "I had a similar thought. Balbus might be so angered by Braymar's escape, he could send legionaries to cause havoc before the morning."

"But we will be no match for a Noxeran force armed with vidiums," added Calute.

"So, Varl, do we comply and allow six Karns to go to an almost certain death?" asked Marcella.

Varl scratched his head. "I think I'd better look at Braymar's pump house plans first. With the information he has collected, let's see if we are in any position to formulate a plan of attack."

Chapter 15

Keela chattered excitedly as she led Matt and Targon down the corridors of Area 5. Matt felt sick. The seafood buffet had been so good that he had gorged on everything in sight and now regretted it bitterly. In an effort to forget about his upset stomach, he turned his attention to the bright red lettering on the curved silver walls. The memories of his first frightening minutes in Karn came flooding back. This time he had an identification chip, and he knew Sorrol. It felt as though he had been in Karn for months instead of just a few days.

"What's so dangerous about Area 5?" Matt asked, tracing the word "DANGER" with his finger as he had done before.

"Nothing much," replied Keela. "Not any more, anyway. It used to be the part of the research lab that contained the chemical and explosives storerooms. We still have one such place for emergencies, but the quantities of explosives are small compared to what was originally here."

"Where are we going?" asked Targon. "I left the food because you said you had something cool to show us."

"I wanted you to see my special place—where I come to think or write sometimes," she said.

"Oh," said Targon, unable to hide his disappointment.

"My generation is very low in numbers," Keela continued. "I do not have many friends my age, and adults do not want to spend time with me."

Matt sensed her sorrow. "Yeah, it's nice to hang out with friends," he agreed. "Why *are* there so few Karns your age?"

"When Balbus arrived with his army fifteen years ago, the future of Karn was uncertain. Adults lived in daily fear, and no one knew what to expect. For several years, until the situation was accepted and it became obvious that nothing immediate was going to happen, few children were born. I am one of the few."

"So, let's see this special place," said Matt. He smiled broadly and tried to convey his enthusiasm now that he understood how important this was to Keela.

"Yes, I'd like that, too," said Targon, following Matt's lead.

Keela came to a door, like any other in the corridor. It was unmarked. She paused and raised her identification chip to the wall pad. The door slid slowly back into the wall. Matt waited for Keela to turn on the lights, but she didn't. They stepped inside. The door closed behind them, cutting off the light from the corridor. It was pitch black. As his eyes adjusted to the darkness of his new environment he began to make out the outline of steel supports, which curved into a dome in front of him.

"This way," said Keela, taking Matt's hand with her left and Targon's with her right. "We are going to climb up two steps and sit on some cushions."

She helped them clamber up onto a circular padded seat. Matt's eyes began to focus. He realized that he was sitting inside an enormous glass ball, that protruded out into the ocean.

"Are you comfortable?" Keela asked, a hint of excitement

in her voice.

"Sure," said Matt.

"Me too," mumbled Targon.

"Okay, here we go."

Keela fumbled below the cushions. Seconds later the ocean floor was illuminated brightly. Matt gasped in awe as brightly colored fish, of species too numerous to count, darted close to the glass. It seemed he could reach out and touch them.

"Too cool," said Targon, Matt's vocabulary now part of his own.

"You mean, 'way too cool'," added Matt, his eyes totally focused on the marine life.

"If we wait long enough, we will probably be able to see some sharks, too," said Keela.

"Great!" said Matt. He could tell by the excitement in Keela's voice that she was delighted that they were enjoying the experience.

She began to identify various types of fish and pointed excitedly as a tiger shark approached. Matt recoiled from the window as the intimidating creature swam past.

After several minutes of observation, Keela knelt up and pressed her face close to the glass. "Do you see that?" she asked.

"What?" asked Matt and Targon together.

"Those lights—over there."

Matt strained to see where she was pointing. There were indeed several sets of flickering lights in the distance.

"Where are they coming from?" he asked.

"This room faces the airlock in Noxeran Area 7. You

may remember me saying that it is the only airlock in Karn big enough for submarine docking."

"So, it's not unusual to see lights?" asked Matt, wondering why he read panic in her voice. "The Noxerans must receive supplies or switch shifts of legionaries frequently."

"Yes, but one sub at a time. A sub arrives, goes into the airlock, docks and usually stays twenty-four hours before leaving. Count the lights. I think there are at least three submarines circling."

"What do you think is going on?" asked Targon.

Keela scrambled off the platform. "I do not know—but it cannot be good. We had better tell Braymar and Calute right now. Something is happening over there."

Keela quickly opened the door. The light that flooded in from the corridor lit the way for Matt and Targon to make a hasty exit.

Matt rubbed his eyes, trying to adjust to the harsh light. "Do you think Balbus has brought reinforcements from Noxera, and they're going to storm this half of Karn?" he asked, as they ran back along the corridor.

"It is what I suspect," she replied, catching her breath. "I just hope we are wrong."

* * * * *

Varl studied the small map that lay on the table in the Elders' meeting chamber. The diagrams were roughly drawn, but understandable. Braymar had done a good job in a limited time and under extremely difficult conditions.

"Does it make sense to you?" Braymar asked. He hovered close by as Varl studied his pencil drawings.

Calute and Marcella sat quietly at the other end of the table.

Varl pursed his lips. He peered closer, using a pen to point at the shapes. "I assume that these rectangles indicate water pumps and that these cylinders represent the turbines that drive the generators?"

Braymar nodded. "Noisy place, that pump house. You can see I even marked the lagged pipes that keep the steam hot."

"I see that you only labeled *two* lagged pipes connected to *two* generators," said Varl. "Where were the others positioned?"

"Others?"

"With this many pumps, there have to be more generators."

Braymar raised his eyebrows and shook his head. "I am sure that I carefully marked the position of *every* piece of equipment in the room."

"Could there be a secondary pump house?"

Braymar shook his head a second time. "I made many visits to Area 6 over the last few years, and I know every room, door and store cupboard. Believe me—there is only the one pump house."

"Odd," muttered Varl. "Really odd." He put down the pen and rubbed his chin. "If the Noxerans are using so many pumps and using such a huge quantity of water, you would imagine they would need a larger number of generators—otherwise, why bother? What's the point of heating the water over the fault line and creating such a large quantity of steam if they're not going to use it to generate more electricity?"

Braymar shrugged. "What else would you pump water for?" he asked.

Varl turned white. "Oh, my!" he said, leaving his mouth gaping. "Oh my, oh my! That's it! That explains the Earth tremors. I sincerely hope I'm wrong."

"What?" asked Calute. "What about the tremors?"

Varl didn't answer. He leaned over the table and stared at the drawing one more time. He knew that he had to be absolutely certain before pursuing this dreadful line of thought.

"Varl, you have alarmed me. *What* do you suspect the Noxerans are doing?" Marcella demanded.

Varl avoided an answer to the question. Instead he chose to ask another. "Where are you holding the Noxeran legionary that we brought back in the submersible?"

"He is under guard here in Area 1," replied Marcella.

"I need to see him immediately! If the legionary knows what's good for him—he'll talk. If he confirms my suspicions, we're all in serious trouble."

"I will take you to see him now," said Calute without hesitation.

Varl followed Calute to the door. He turned back to look at Braymar. "You did a great job. I'm sorry to be vague at this point. I need you to find five trustworthy Karns and meet Calute and I back here in thirty minutes."

"Done," said Braymar.

"Marcella, can you locate the original drawings of the

pump house from when Karn was built, and find out about any modifications that were made before the Noxerans arrived?"

She looked bewildered. "I will do my best—but will you not tell us what you suspect?"

Varl sighed. "There's no time. I'll explain everything when we get back—*if* I find my conclusions are correct. Let's hope that for once, I'm wrong!"

* * * * *

Varl was nervous. By the time they had traveled the short distance to the temporary prison, he knew deep inside that his deductions were correct. Visiting the legionary was necessary simply to confirm his suspicions and prove his theory to the Karns. He watched Calute hold up his identification chip to the pad and punch in a code to unlock the extra electronic bolt on the door. Calute instructed the Karn guard posted outside to remain vigilant while he and Varl interviewed the Noxeran prisoner.

Calute entered, but remained at the back of the room. Varl took a deep breath and approached the young man, who lay on his bed facing the wall. He pulled up a chair and sat down cautiously—unsure of the response he would get to his questions. The Noxeran legionary failed to turn his head in acknowledgement of his visitors. Varl decided to begin talking to his back.

"I trust that you are being treated well," said Varl, hopeful of a reply. There was none. "In return for the compassion we showed to you in the airlock, I hope that you will provide some answers to my questions."

The young man remained stoically positioned on the bed. Varl waited a few seconds and, when there was no response, continued undeterred.

"Keela saved you from drowning, and I saved your life a second time by bringing you with us when the airlock was flooding. Surely, you can see that we are trustworthy and compassionate individuals. We mean you no harm."

Varl sighed. There was still no response—not a twitch of a muscle nor a movement of a limb.

"Well, if he won't cooperate I guess he'll drown with us at the hands of Balbus," said Varl, rising from the chair. His comment had been deliberate. It caused the desired reaction by the prisoner.

A feeble voice whispered, "Drown?" The legionary rolled over and studied Varl, who sat down once again by the edge of the bed.

"Yes, drown," Varl repeated. "I need to hear from you why Balbus has been pumping water in excess of the amount needed for the energy he has been generating. You and I both know that there are many more pumps than generators. So what is he doing with the excess water being pumped into the fault if he is not generating electricity and sending it to the mainland?"

The legionary looked pale, and his eyes had the sunken look of a man who had lost everything. He shook his head. "It is more than my life is worth to give you that information."

"While I understand your fear of the consequences of turning against your own people . . ."

"What do you understand?" the young man suddenly

came to life. He sat up and snapped, "You understand nothing! Balbus would at best cut out my tongue, and probably execute me as a traitor. My family would disown me, and I could never return to Noxera even if I did survive."

"You may not have a family or a Noxera to return to!" said Varl, sufficiently raising his voice to label the point. "And nor will there be a Realm of Karn!"

The legionary seemed dazed by Varl's brutal truth. "The Princeps has promised us a new Noxera." The words flowed fast and furious in defense of his leader and his beliefs. "His loyal followers will have a position of command in either the Princeps' new army or the new Noxeran Senate. My family will be proud that I stood up for freedom from tyranny."

Varl's eyes narrowed. He spoke slowly and clearly, inches from the young man's face. "And how does Balbus intend to carry out such a coup with so small an army?"

"I am not permitted to divulge such information."

"And will you divulge the information and confirm my theory if I prove to you that your family may be at risk, and that Balbus is nothing but a dishonest con-artist intent upon tyrannical control?"

"Nonius Balbus would not cause harm to the families of his supporters. His plan is carefully devised to cause panic and a threat of future destruction of Noxera so that the present government will resign."

"By causing a massive earthquake?"

The legionary seemed stunned by Varl's insight. He counteracted immediately. "A controlled earthquake that would cause enough damage to make his point clearly."

Varl leaned forward and whispered, "And what about the

tidal waves caused by this earthquake?"

The legionary was silent. He opened his mouth as if he were about to reply and then closed it tightly.

"I thought as much," said Varl. "Balbus has not been entirely honest with you. I suspect that only a handful of his closest Senate members are privy to the true information and the extent of the damage that will be caused by his plan."

Calute neared the bed, an expression of concern on his face. Varl thought that his golden complexion seemed a shade lighter. The news had not been welcome.

Varl reached up and touched Calute's arm. "I'm sorry," he said quietly. "My theory is that Balbus had no intention of generating more electricity. He built the extra pumps to send a huge quantity of water into the fault line at its weakest points. There would be such a huge build-up of hot steam, heated by the Earth's core and unable to escape to the surface, that an explosion would occur and cause a massive earthquake. Tidal waves would follow. With only fifty miles between Karn and the shore, Noxera would be devastated and probably flooded. All who live on the coastal plains within one hundred miles of the principality would drown."

"And Karn?" Calute asked, his voice trembling.

"I can only guess . . ." began Varl, "but I fear that Karn will be unable to stand the severe tremors caused by an earthquake of such magnitude."

"Why? Why would he do this?" screamed the legionary.

"It seems a perfect plan to wipe out his enemies and those civilians who would not support a new regime based on Roman traditions," suggested Varl. "Then he, as the next Caesar, would build a new Noxera with no opposition and only loyal followers."

"What guarantees would he have that his loyal followers would stay loyal after such destruction and death?" asked Calute.

"I imagine that he'd claim it a natural disaster," replied Varl. "I'm sure there would be some survivors, and he'd have sent his loyal citizens to higher ground. In times of tragedy, the people who have lost everything turn to a strong leader. Balbus would be there to clean up and rebuild, offer support and claim the whole thing a freak of nature. Those few legionaries who know better and announce otherwise would be silenced immediately. The rest would follow Balbus for fear of their own lives and because there is no alternative."

"Okay, enough!" the legionary interrupted. "I confirm that you are correct. But Balbus swore to us all that the scientists had calculated the water flow accurately, and that testing had been done for so many years that our families would not be at risk."

"And you really thought it could be done to such a precise degree?" Calute stared at him, his mouth gaping. "To tamper successfully with the Earth's crust is no easy feat. There are *no* guarantees when you are messing with nature."

"When you live in hardship caused by bad harvests and years of drought, and your family is constantly hungry, you will believe anyone who offers you hope for the future and a better life," shouted the legionary, perhaps trying to defend how gullible he had been.

"But the Noxeran government is popular and democratic," said Calute.

"When did you last visit Noxera?" asked the legionary.

"In the last thirty years Karn has become a forgotten world—cut off from the mainland and self-sufficient. You are out of touch. Noxera has changed dramatically. The rich have become richer, and the poor have nothing. Unemployment is high and surviving from day to day is a struggle."

"But Balbus is *not* the answer," said Varl adamantly. "Surely you can see that he is at best, evil, and at worst, insane? He's in this for power and glory and will cause death and destruction along the way. You will be substituting one badly managed government for another even more corrupt. What has the Princeps told you of his plans to reform the economy and create jobs?"

"Nothing." The legionary hung his head. "Okay, you needn't say any more. I'm convinced by your arguments. I thank you for your compassion and I'll help you. Tell me what you need to know."

Varl slapped him on the back. "You won't have any regrets. You'll go home a hero, I promise."

"Enough of the soft talk," Calute snapped. "We have a matter of hours to stop Balbus, so let us get on with it!"

Chapter 16

Keela ran clumsily into the Elders' meeting chamber with Matt and Targon close behind. "Where is Calute?" she panted.

"He will be here with Varl shortly," Marcella snapped. "I suggest you take a seat and enter this room in a more respectful manner next time, young lady."

"This can't wait, Marcella," said Matt, gasping. "Do you know where they are?"

"Here," said Calute, stepping through the parting doors. "What is the problem?"

Keela rushed forward. "Balbus is going to attack! There will be hundreds more legionaries here any minute. How are we going to stop him?"

Calute raised his eyebrows. "How do you know this, Keela?"

"There are several submarines circling outside the airlock in Area 7. We have just come back from Area 5 and the submarine lights were plainly visible from one of the observation lookouts."

"It's true," interrupted Matt. "We all saw at least three of them. There's no doubt that the lights were from submarines." He directed his gaze at Varl. "This is our chance to *free the people of Karn,*" he stressed the words from his game. "Do you have a good defensive plan—or better still, one of attack?"

Varl winked at him. Matt knew that Varl had understood his deeper meaning.

"We may not need one," Varl replied calmly.

"May not need one?" shouted Keela, her voice still quivering. "Without some kind of plan, we will never fight off Balbus and his legionaries. They will storm through the pod chute, take the five Karns they demanded, and recapture Braymar. Who knows what other destruction they might cause!"

Calute placed his hand on her shoulder and rubbed it gently as if trying to calm her. "Thank you for the information, Keela, but we will not be needing a plan to fend off the Noxerans."

Matt screwed up his face and looked at Varl for an answer.

"Not be needing one?" questioned Keela, her voice rising sharply.

Targon slapped his thighs. "I just don't get you," he said, glaring angrily at Varl. "When have you ever sat back and accepted defeat?"

Varl gave a weak smile. "Never . . . and I don't intend to now. Calute and I have been talking with the captured legionary. Balbus and his army are not getting reinforcements, they are all leaving."

"Leaving?" questioned Keela. "The legionary *really* said that?"

"He did indeed," confirmed Calute.

"Why would they do that?" asked Matt.

Varl opened his mouth to reply, but then stared at Keela,

who began dancing around excitedly.

"We are free! We are actually free of them!" She threw her arms first around Targon and then Matt. "Freedom! The word sounds so wonderful. I will sing it over and over until I believe it. Freedom, free . . ."

Marcella pushed back her chair and slammed her hand on the table. "Enough of this!" she screamed.

Stunned by the noise, Keela stopped her celebrating and turned to look at Marcella.

The Elder's golden skin had taken on a purple tinge. Her arms, supporting her as she bent over the table, shook noticeably. "Calute? Varl? Thirty minutes ago we all appeared to be doomed and you offered no explanation when you hurried off to see the prisoner. I waited patiently for you to return and did as you asked. The pump house plans are here. Now you do not show any happiness by this news of the Noxerans' departure, so I can only deduce that all is *not* well. I have waited long enough. I want explanations, now!"

"I'm sorry, Marcella, for keeping you in the dark," said Varl. "I had to be sure that my deductions were correct before I caused alarm. Sit down everyone. Marcella is right. The news is not good, and we have a lot of work to do."

Matt watched Keela's expression turn from sheer joy to utter despair. He pulled back a heavy chair and sat in silence next to her, waiting for Varl to deliver the bad news. Braymar entered with several volunteers and took the remaining seats around the table.

Varl remained standing. "I see no pleasant way to break this news to you. Karn will be destroyed in less than twenty-four hours if we cannot find a solution to stop the Princeps' plan."

"But, you just said the Noxerans were leaving." Keela jumped in.

Varl glared at her and put his finger to his lips. Keela folded her arms and sat back in her chair.

"Indeed they are. They are leaving in order to get a safe distance away from Karn before it is destroyed by a huge earthquake."

This time Marcella interrupted. "And just how do they know that such an earthquake will occur in the next twenty-four hours? Unless . . ." Her voice trailed off.

Varl nodded. "I can see, Marcella, that you are beginning to put the pieces together. Balbus has *not* been supplying extra electricity to the mainland. It was all a cover for the real purpose of his being here. The holes he bored deep into the Earth's crust along the fault line will be pumped full of water until the pressure from trapped steam causes an almighty explosion and triggers the earthquake. He has been practicing with minor tremors recently, which you have experienced."

Keela gasped. She grabbed her hair so tightly that Matt thought she would wrench it from her scalp.

"But how can they time an earthquake so exactly?" asked Marcella. "Doesn't someone have to stay to oversee the operation?"

"Computer," mumbled Matt. "They'll do it by computer."

Calute cleared his throat and twirled the ends of his mustache as he grunted his reply. "The boy is correct. The whole operation will be cleverly controlled by one massive computer."

"And I have had the horrible fortune to see it—or should I say *her*," added Braymar. "It is a computer unlike anything I have ever seen. I watched her interact with one of the programmers on one of my spying missions. She has a voice and a mind of her own—very argumentative, too. If I had realized her significance before, I would have attempted to get a closer look at the system."

Matt leaned close to Varl and whispered, "The computer has to be the Keeper! The life of everyone in Karn is at risk from her destructive program. It's not Nonius Balbus at all. Remember the last lines of the poem?"

Varl nodded. "'*Destroying the Keeper, simple it seems, can hurt those you love and end your dreams.*' I *was* puzzled by that—now it seems plain."

"I guess it means that we can't take the easy option and use explosives to destroy the computer and prevent it from running the program," Matt sighed.

"I would have to agree with you. That solution is too obvious," mumbled Varl.

"Did I hear you say that you have a solution?" asked Marcella, leaning over the table.

"I'm afraid not. Matt was just saying that the obvious solution of blowing up the computer was *not* an option," said Varl, thinking quickly.

"Why not?" said Braymar. "It is the only way out, if you ask me. Destroy the computer and we destroy the program."

"Because destruction of the computer doesn't necessarily mean the plan will be halted," said Varl. "Balbus is too clever. He has just spent fifteen years planning and preparing for this event. Only a fool would not have allowed for our obvious reaction and created a back-up plan. I suspect that the computer is holding the valves shut. If that is the case, and we destroy the computer, the valves may automatically open and we would have no way of shutting them off and halting the flow of water."

Calute continued. "Do you think there may be a way that we can break into the computer program and stop it?"

"Possibly," said Varl. "Although it won't be easy. You'd better bring me up-to-date with your techbox. Let's hope the Noxeran system isn't complicated and that with Matt's computer knowledge we can work out a way."

"What about tackling the problem from two directions?" suggested Braymar.

Varl raised his eyebrows. "What have you in mind?"

"I saw the water pipes from the pump house when I swam back with Keela. There are nine or ten, laid above ground on the seabed. Each pipe is at least two feet in diameter. It might be possible to cut through them before they reach the wells in the fault line."

". . . and attempt to divert the water back into the sea before it is channeled into the holes," clarified Varl, mulling the idea over. "An interesting idea. It might be possible, but it would take heavy lifting equipment or industrial cutting tools."

"We have underwater cutting torches, which we have used for repairs to the oxygen scrubbing system," said Calute. "It would not take long to get a team of Karns out there to try."

"But it would take too long to cut through so many pipes

that large—and time is short," Varl reasoned.

"Explosives . . ." said Braymar. "It may not be a good idea to blow up the computer, but there is no reason why we cannot have a carefully controlled explosion to demolish the water pipes."

A loud rumbling broke into the conversation. The table shook violently, and Keela clutched the arms of her chair for support. Varl watched as water in the glasses around the table slopped onto the polished surface.

Calute took Marcella's hand and squeezed it tightly. Tears welled in his eyes. "Forget the computer and forget the water pipes—we are too late to save Karn! Balbus has already won!"

Chapter 17

Matt clutched the arms of his chair as it vibrated beneath his body. He saw fear in the faces of those gathered around the table. He looked up at the ceiling. No cracks had appeared, and there was no indication that it was about to give way. His eyes fell on Varl who seemed surprisingly unruffled, considering his world was about to end. Focusing on the calmness of Varl's demeanor made Matt feel suddenly hopeful that all was not lost.

"It's not the same sound as before," said Varl, as if hearing Matt's thoughts. "Listen, Calute."

Calute nodded. "It does sound a little different."

"Besides, Balbus would never have succeeded in evacuating several hundred people in such a short space of time." As Varl reached the end of his sentence, the rumbling and shaking subsided. "There, I was right—it wasn't Earth tremors," he said proudly.

The entire event had lasted but a few seconds. Everyone relaxed, taking deep breaths and exhaling audibly. Calm returned to the room and puzzled faces turned to look at Varl.

"What do you think it was, if it wasn't Earth tremors?" asked Matt.

"A controlled explosion. I'd say that the Noxerans have just eliminated our only means of getting across to the other half of Karn."

Marcella leaped from her seat. "You think they have destroyed the only connecting pod chute? What evil men are these? They guarantee us a certain death, trapping us in this half."

Varl's expression was grim for the first time. "And my guess is that they will also make the emergency airlocks inoperable before they leave, so that we can't enter the Noxeran half by using the submersible."

"But they do not know the secret of the Karn people," said Keela, sounding cheerful. "We can always swim across to Area 6 to reach the computer."

Calute shook his head. "Our secret is of little use. If all of the airlocks have been sealed by the Noxerans, we have no means of getting inside. And even if we could, Varl and Matt would not be able to come without access to a decompression chamber. We need them. None of us here possess the computer knowledge that these two travelers share. It seems that Braymar's idea of cutting the water pipes is our only hope."

"Not so," said Braymar, sporting a large grin, which broadened by the minute. "I know a way to get Varl and Matt across to Area 6."

Calute raised his eyebrows. "Well, tell us! You have had one good idea today. Let's hear another."

"I have had this route in the back of my mind for months as a possible method for a surprise attack. We can use the pod chute between Area 1 and Area 6."

"I was told that the Noxerans flooded it years ago," said Varl, quickly challenging the idea.

Braymar pushed back his chair, walked to the other end

of the table, and positioned himself between Varl and Calute. He lowered his head to their level and continued in a tantalizing tone. "And they did. They removed the pod and flooded the chute with sea water. But . . . the chute itself is intact and the pressure inside remains at sea level, the same as the air within Karn."

Matt felt a sudden rush of excitement, as he understood what Braymar was getting at. "If the pressure is at sea level, Varl and I wouldn't need a decompression chamber!"

"Correct. The pod chute doors were left open during the flooding and we have diving equipment. We unseal the doors at the top of the stairwell and climb down to where the level of the water has flooded the stairs. Keela and Sorrol could lead you across. I estimate it would take no more than twelve minutes to swim the length of the chute."

Varl smiled. "Excellent, Braymar. I actually think we have two plans again. I would need instructions as to the location of the computer and the pump house within Area 6."

"Certainly. I can show you on the old plans that Marcella found. But, there *is* one minor problem . . ."

"Which is?" asked Varl.

"We have no idea how the Noxerans sealed the doors at the top of the stairwell on their side of the pod chute. You would have to carry cutting equipment and a variety of tools."

Varl nodded. "Don't worry—we'll find a way. I suggest we collect equipment together and then catch a few hours' sleep. I'm exhausted from today's earlier adventures. Anyway, we need to allow time for the Noxerans to evacuate the area completely."

Calute got to his feet eagerly. "Agreed. Let us begin

preparations. Varl, you will lead the expedition to Area 6. Braymar, I will organize explosives for your team and cutting tools for Varl's group while you all get some sleep. Marcella, find the radio headsets so that we can all stay in contact. We begin our operations at midnight."

Matt looked around at the smiling faces as everyone began to leave the room. Minutes earlier they had all thought their lives were at an end. He had seen so much fear. Now, excited chatter and hope for the future prevailed. Despair had been replaced with optimism.

* * * * *

Varl fingered the small airpack gingerly. "Not what I had in mind," he grunted, strapping it to his back. "Are you sure this thing works?"

"In my home," said Matt with apprehension,"diving gear consists of huge air tanks connected by breathing apparatus—nothing as lightweight and compact as this." He picked up the triangular breathing mask, wondering how something that would barely cover his nose and mouth could work efficiently.

Keela smiled. "Your airpacks will work well, do not worry."

"I checked them out personally," added Sorrol, who looked quite amused by Varl's sudden pessimism. "I will not let you drown!"

"Just be thankful they are so compact. You will not even notice them on your back," said Calute, watching the proceedings. "The headsets have been designed to work in conjunction with the scuba equipment. There is a small microphone in the mask so that we can also hear you. Keela and Sorrol have adapted versions with a microphone that lowers automatically for speaking."

Varl's eyes twinkled. "Fascinating! I must take time to study both devices when I return. I'm always interested in new technology."

"Wish I were a Piscean," said Matt. "It must be great to do away with the breathing apparatus altogether."

Varl sighed. "I agree. We're already going to be weighed down with the cutting tools." He looked at the large container on the floor.

"Do not worry, Keela and Sorrol will be able to manage the equipment with ease," said Calute, meeting his gaze. He moved toward the stairwell. "Are you ready? The doors at this end of the pod chute were unsealed while you slept."

Varl nodded. "Okay, I'm ready."

"Me too," said Matt.

"Good. Keep your headsets turned on at all times. They will work underwater too—just in case you have any difficulty swimming across." Calute shook Varl's hand. "Good luck, my friend Varl. I am eternally grateful that you and the two young men had the good fortune to arrive in Karn. I am sorry that I showed you so much mistrust in the beginning. You have more than proven your loyalty to my people."

Varl smiled. "I understand your skepticism under the circumstances, Calute. We're grateful to you for your hospitality and friendship, and glad that we're able to help each other."

"You will never know *how* grateful," muttered Matt.

While Sorrol and Calute manually opened the doors and wedged them apart with a steel rod, Varl whispered, "Okay, Matt, my boy. Let's do what we came here to do. Let's *win* the game and get home."

Matt grinned. "Win? I'm aiming for the high score!"

Varl laughed.

They followed Keela down two levels until they met water covering the top step of the bottom flight of stairs. Sorrol picked up the container in his strong arms and quickly caught up with the group. As the water washed over their bare feet, Matt and Varl pulled their masks down over their faces. Keela showed them how to adjust the controls and start the flow of air. She picked up the other end of the large container and led the way into the chute with Sorrol at her side.

Matt felt a moment of panic as he stepped into the glass tunnel and the water covered his head. Air did not seem to be reaching him from the airpack! He fought for a few breaths and grabbed Varl's sleeve in alarm. Sorrol turned and looked behind. The Piscean held up three fingers of his free hand and counted slowly. Matt tried to remain calm. He focused on Sorrol. After a few seconds a supply of fresh air found its way into Matt's lungs, and he was able to relax for the journey across.

* * * * *

Braymar led a team of four out of the airlock in Area 1. Among the carefully selected group were two detonation experts and a mechanical engineer. Each wore a headset to allow hands-free communications underwater.

Braymar was grateful for the genetic mutations that allowed their ease of movement in the water. Never had he felt so free. Until now, their secret had been closely guarded for fear that the Noxerans would use Karns as divers to speed up their project. Their large webbed feet propelled them along rapidly, and the water seemed as natural an environment as dry land. Had the Karns not developed into true Pisceans, today's task would have been impossible.

Braymar steered the powered microsub containing the explosives toward the water pipes that he had seen earlier in the day. Ten large pipelines, laid closely together, carried the water from the pump house In Area 6 across leveled underwater terrain and toward the bored wells.

The microsub, a lightweight cylinder, three feet long and with a steering bar at one end, was easy to maneuver into position. Braymar swam behind the apparatus, lightly touching the controls as needed and steering it in the right direction. He led the group for twenty minutes, following the pipes until he reached the point where they divided. He turned off the power and allowed the microsub to rest on the ocean floor.

Braymar beckoned to the other divers to close in. He unlatched the top half of the microsub, opening it to reveal four mesh carriers, each packed with a supply of explosives, timing devices and flashlights. The immediate area was brightly illuminated by the powerful floodlights of Karn. But out by the wells, the range of vision would be a few feet.

He looked at his watch. It was already 1:05. Varl had recommended that they finish by 4 a.m. to allow time for evacuation, in case both teams failed in their missions. Failure, he thought, was not a word he used. Besides, where would they go? And how far did Varl assume they could swim in a few hours? Certainly not far enough away from the effects of a major earthquake! Failure was not an option. They would all die if at least one team did not succeed.

The next move was vital. Braymar swam over the pipes inspecting each carefully. He spoke into his radio headset to the other divers.

"We must not damage the original two pipelines. If we destroy all ten, electricity generation will be disrupted, and Karn will be without power."

He looked closely at two corroded pipes in the middle. There could be no doubt that they were years older than the other eight.

"At this point the pipes divide, and each leads to a separate well. The middle two must remain operational. Even though it would be easier, we cannot plant the explosives here, where they are close together. We will have to destroy each pipe individually before it reaches the well. Take two pipes each, follow them to the wellhead, and set the explosives between thirty and fifty feet back from the fault line. Make sure that you destroy any remaining drilling equipment. We do not want the Noxerans back to try again." Braymar looked at his watch. "Allow two hours on the timers. Detonation time to be 3:15 a.m. Meet back here in one hour and be on the lookout for sharks. Any questions?"

The divers indicated that all was understood. They collected their packs from the open hold of the microsub and swam off in different directions. The wells were at least two hundred yards apart. As long as the explosives were set accurately, there would be no risk to the original two pipes. Braymar accompanied the least experienced team member to the first bore. He watched him painstakingly place the explosives and set the timer. The massive metal structure of the drilling rig lay idle to the side.

"Attach a second device to one of the rig supports," Braymar instructed. "I want nothing left that is of any use to the Noxerans."

The explosives secured, Braymar's team returned to the meeting point. Two other divers had beaten them back. Braymar closed the microsub, now empty of its valuable cargo. Confident of success, he radioed Calute to inform him that the task was almost complete.

Ten minutes passed. The fourth member of the team, Eriks, had still not returned. A group of sharks swam ominously close. Braymar removed the stunner from the clip on the side of the microsub and passed it to one of the others.

He looked at his watch anxiously and contacted Calute through his headset. "I do not like this. Eriks may be in trouble, and time is running out. I will take the microsub and look for him."

He reached for the controls to power up the microsub. His hand had barely touched the steering when a loud boom shook the ground. The deafening sound reverberated around his head, sending a chill down his spine. He looked up to see large chunks of rock and drilling equipment hurtling toward them.

"Hit the seabed!" he hollered.

Braymar lunged for a small rock entrenched in the ocean floor. He grabbed hold, moving his head downward between his arms. Sand and fragments of coral whipped across his body, cutting into the exposed parts of his skin. Shards of metal tore his garments and cut his legs. The power of the water currents caused by the shock waves pushed him sideways, spinning and tumbling him along the rocky ocean floor. The microsub hurtled after him, tossed in the current as if it were a toy.

"What's happening? Braymar . . . Braymar . . . answer me!" Calute yelled over the radio.

When the debris began to settle, Braymar struggled to swim back in search of the others. With sore limbs, every stroke was painful. The microsub lay battered on the bottom. Three members of the team emerged from different directions, bruised and distressed, but each in one piece. The fourth, Eriks, had still not returned.

Braymar adjusted the volume in his headset and responded to Calute's frantic call. "Some of the explosives detonated prematurely. I am afraid we have lost Eriks," he announced sadly. "He could not have survived the blast. I suspect faulty equipment is to blame. Those timing devices had been sitting in Area 5 for years."

"Get out of there, now!" Calute ordered. "Get the rest of the team back here. There is no telling if the other explosives will detonate prematurely. One life lost is one too many."

Chapter 18

Matt clambered up the steps at the end of the pod chute and tried to remove his mask. It fit snugly on his face. He had to pull hard to break the suction. He sat on the floor and took a few minutes to breathe in the fresh air before pulling out a small cloth from inside his rubberized suit. He wiped his face and toweled his dripping hair. Varl had already surfaced. Matt sat next to him, breathing heavily.

"It took fourteen minutes to swim across," said Matt, glancing at his watch.

"Then Braymar wasn't far off," replied Varl, getting to his feet. "Especially as we stopped to sort out your airpack."

Sorrol and Keela were already examining the seal around the door into Area 6.

"What do you think?" asked Varl, fingering the putty-like substance. "Any quick way to break the seal?"

Sorrol sighed. "The bad news is that we are not familiar with this Noxeran sealant. The good news is that we brought a laser-torch to cut through the metal of the door. It will just take longer."

Keela opened the container and handed the heavy equipment to Sorrol. Matt passed him a protective mask.

"I suggest you all stand well away. This is going to take a while." Sorrol set to work, hardly allowing them time to move back.

Matt watched as the powerful beam cut a thin line inside the frame of the door. He felt excited yet nervous as Sorrol completed the large circle and put down the laser. Would they be able to destroy the Keeper of the Realm and free the Karns before Nonius Balbus succeeded with his horrific plan?

As Sorrol and Varl began to push on the metal, Matt moved closer in anticipation. The cut section of the door reverberated with a loud clang as it hit the floor in Area 6.

"Let us go!" shouted Sorrol, picking up the equipment and shoving it through the gaping hole before him.

Varl struggled to raise his legs high enough to get through the opening. Matt scrambled over after Keela.

It was quiet on the other side. As Matt stood up and looked to see why Sorrol hadn't started down the corridor, the pointed end of a vidium dug into his chest. Matt stared in horror at two Noxeran guards who blocked his route. He recognized both.

Matt raised his hands in compliance and inched closer to Varl.

Carella smiled wryly. "So, young Marcus and Senator Varl, we meet again. The Princeps warned us that you would attempt to gain access to Area 6."

Argus took a step forward and pointed his vidium at Varl's head. "You will never make a fool of me again!" he sneered.

"We need your help," said Varl, showing no indication of fear. He stared down the deadly black throat of the weapon. "We are all in danger."

Carella laughed from deep within his belly. The sinister sound echoed down the corridor. "Help is the *last* thing you will get from us! My hearing may be permanently damaged after the last stunt that you pulled," he spat. "My ears are still ringing."

"I trusted you," said Argus. "You turned me into a laughingstock. Do you think I will ever listen to anything else you have to say?"

"Carella, Argus, I beg you," began Sorrol.

"You beg me?" Carella laughed again. His face twisted into an expression of sheer hatred. "Then get down on your knees and beg even harder!"

Matt followed the others and quickly knelt on the cold floor at Carella's feet.

"Sir . . . " said Keela bravely.

Carella placed the vidium on Keela's cheek and traced a line with it from her chin to her knees. "I've been called Legionary Carella and Vault Guard Carella, but never *sir*. Stand up, girl!"

"Don't you touch her," shouted Matt, quickly rising and placing himself in front of Keela. "She is an innocent Karn, trying to save thousands of lives on the mainland. You show her some respect."

Carella took a step backward and eyed Matt with astonishment. "My! We do have two heroic youngsters. You had better explain why you would need to save thousands of lives on the mainland."

"Because Noxera will be soon be devastated by an earthquake and a massive tidal wave that will surely follow," said Keela, looking Carella boldly in the eyes.

He laughed again. "Why would you think such a thing?"

"Because Nonius Balbus intends to destroy all opposition

to his new senate in Noxera," Matt interjected.

"Balbus is merely planning a small surprise to bring his opposition in line with his way of thinking," Carella replied. "We have seen a sample of minor quakes over the last few months. The Princeps has the situation well under control."

Varl, still on his knees, tried to reason with Carella. "We have proof. The quantity of water being pumped into the wells that you have drilled will build up such terrific pressure that the earthquake will destroy cities several hundred miles from here. Noxera will be in ruins, your family members will perish, and Balbus will take control. Without a large army, he has few ways that he can achieve this. What better way than to wipe out thousands who might rise up against him under the guise of a natural disaster?"

Matt could see by Carella's changing expression that Varl had captured his attention. Argus was difficult to read. He stood to attention, vidium still raised, a blank look on his face.

"Why would the Princeps bring harm to those in Noxera who favor him?" Carella asked.

"And how many do you suppose that is?" Varl retorted. "How many Noxerans wish to have a tyrannical ruler? Balbus' idea of a Roman style of government can hardly be described as democratic. His senators will be handpicked, not voted in. The present Noxeran government may be disliked, but at least it's *truly* democratic."

Varl got off his knees and rubbed his back as he stood upright. "Balbus will have already ordered the stealing of valuables and treasures from banks and museums, and will have sent his known supporters and their families into the hills for safety. In a few hours the rest will perish, and I assure you that life for those who survive will be more difficult under Balbus!"

Matt added, "If you stay here, you certainly won't be around to see it."

Carella turned to face Matt, his face drained of blood. "More lies!" he screamed. "Everything you have ever said to me has been a lie!"

Varl continued undeterred. "Karn cannot withstand an earthquake of such magnitude. We will all die. We are too close to the fault line."

"Balbus said . . ."

"Balbus told you what, Carella? Did you seriously think he could tamper with the Earth's crust and control the results so precisely?" asked Varl.

"He left me in command here . . . to see that everything ran according to plan. I am to be promoted to Commander of the 2nd Legion when the new Noxeran army is established," Carella spluttered.

"And what about you, Argus?" asked Varl. "We heard that you were being sent back to the mainland. Why did Balbus change his mind and leave you here?"

"He has given me a chance to prove myself. Before you tricked me, the Princeps had no reason to fault my work."

"So why has everyone else been evacuated?" questioned Matt.

"Ready to take control on the mainland," Carella replied.

"To get out of danger, more likely!" said Matt, raising his voice.

"Carella, if what you say is true," suggested Varl,

"wouldn't Balbus want his new commander at his side to help set up the new army?"

"Stop! No more!" shouted Carella. He pointed the vidium at Varl. "You fill our heads with nonsense!"

Varl continued his verbal attack. "Think, Carella. Put the pieces together. Why would Balbus need so many pumps and huge water pipes for such a small earthquake? It certainly wasn't to produce electricity. There are no new generators."

"I know the Princeps well. I have worked for him for many years and have been a loyal follower. He wouldn't leave us to die."

"Yes, he would. You failed to stop our plot to release Braymar," taunted Varl. "The Princeps is now punishing you and Argus for your incompetence. He shows no mercy!"

The ground shook.

Keela clutched Matt's sleeve. "Are we too late?"

Sorrol shook his head. "That is not an earthquake. My guess is that Braymar has detonated the explosives. It sounds like a very small explosion, though."

"Then we have to assume he failed to blow up all of the pipes," said Varl, with urgency in his voice. "Carella, Argus, are you with us?"

"With you?" hollered Carella. "Never! I will hear no more lies. You are our prisoners."

"Think again!" shouted Sorrol, the laser torch still in his hands.

He acted swiftly, raising the torch and turning it on to full power. The laser struck Carella's arm. His sleeve burst into flames. He yelled in pain, dropping the vidium to the floor.

Matt seized the opportunity. He dived at Argus' ankles. The guard toppled sideways. His vidium fired as he staggered to maintain his balance, narrowly missing Keela. Varl joined in. He grabbed the guard's wrist, grappling with him for the weapon.

Argus was strong and determined. He kicked at Matt, striking him in the mouth. Matt ignored his bleeding lip and sank his teeth into Argus' ankle. Argus howled and fell to the floor. Varl wrenched the vidium from Argus' hand and directed it at the defeated legionary.

Carella continued to scream. He finally managed to remove his burning shirt. He grimaced in pain as he studied his raw flesh. Sorrol kept the laser torch directed at Carella.

"Keela, pick up Carella's vidium!" shouted Matt, seeing it still at Carella's feet. She plucked the weapon from the floor.

Matt could hardly believe what they had just accomplished. He felt relieved that none of them had been injured.

"If you both value your life, you will help us," said Varl, gasping for breath.

"To do what?" asked Argus.

"To reprogram the computer," said Sorrol.

Carella sank to the floor, the pain obviously too great to bear. "Anything," he said with difficulty. "Just get me help."

"We'll get you a doctor as soon as we're done," said Varl. "If we don't act fast you'll need an undertaker instead." He handed Argus' vidium to Sorrol and took communicators away. "Keep them guarded while Matt and I are at work. Argus, lead the way."

* * * * *

Argus opened the door to the small computer room, located next to the pump house. Matt entered first and approached the computer, bolted in sections to the far wall. He was surprised by how little space it occupied, and by how uncomplicated the system appeared. He sat down in front of a screen that was double the size of the computer. There were no dials or controls—just a small keyboard showing a few colored lights and symbols.

"What do you make of her, Matt, my boy?" Varl asked in a soft voice.

"I'd guess she's in sleep mode at the moment. Let's awaken her memory," said Matt, reaching for the keyboard.

The screen became illuminated. Matt sat back to read the display of programs on the main menu.

"What's your guess?" asked Varl.

"Not sure," Matt mused, licking his bleeding bottom lip as he read the options. "I doubt we'll get access to any of them without a security code."

"Use my sonic encryptor," Carella groaned. "I assume you got hold of one and know how they work, since you managed to turn off the sonic walls."

Sorrol directed a vidium at Carella's head while Varl unclipped the encryptor from his belt.

"The vault computer that controls the sonic wall is networked to this one," explained Carella. He drew in a deep breath and winced in pain. "I wouldn't be surprised if the codes are the same. Please . . . I need a doctor."

Varl smiled. He fingered the tiny silver encryptor and directed it at the computer. "Thank you, Carella. We will get you help as soon as we can," he reassured. "Okay, Matt, my boy, it's your choice. Which program do we go for?"

"Pump house?" Matt suggested.

Varl shook his head. "Too obvious. What else is there?"

Matt read out loud as he thought about each. "The vault room, main airlock, emergency lighting, air purification . . ." Most seemed self-explanatory. His eyes were drawn to the word 'Pompeii.' He pointed to the screen. "I'm willing to bet it's this one," he said.

"You're a bright one," said Varl. "I'll lay odds that you're right. If I remember correctly, Pompeii was a Roman city completely destroyed by the volcano, Vesuvius, in AD 79. Balbus is just the kind of man to show such twisted logic that he would believe his evil plan would have a similar scale of destruction."

Matt's fingers hesitated over the 'Enter' key.

"Do it," whispered Varl. "Time is running out. We've probably only a few hours."

Matt touched the key lightly and waited anxiously as the program loaded. A pair of haunting blue eyes dominated the screen. Narrow and cold, with thin brows that curved dramatically downward, the eyes blinked twice.

"Who wishes to access my database?" a woman's sinister voice asked. The eyes blinked a third time.

Matt felt slightly intimidated by the staring pupils. "Matt wishes to access your database."

The eyes closed and then opened slowly as if considering his request. "My program has been sealed indefinitely to outsiders. I am the Keeper of the database of the Realm of Karn. I will not allow access."

"This is an emergency," continued Matt. "We must rewrite your program immediately."

The eyes closed and opened once more. "My program has been set. Only *I* may change the task for which it has been predetermined and there is no emergency under which this can be done."

Varl moved close to the screen. "I am Varl, a scientist with wisdom and knowledge of the world. We implore you to reconsider this decision. If you do not, thousands of innocent lives will be lost as a direct consequence of your program."

The eyelids flickered for a second and then the haunting blue circles continued to stare at them both. "On what grounds do you base this assumption?"

"Your program is timed to open the valves in water pipes 3-10. Am I correct?"

"Correct. This will happen in precisely twenty-two minutes."

"Twenty-two minutes?" exclaimed Matt.

"Varl, Matt, do something, please!" begged Keela.

Varl touched her arm. "We're working on it in a logical manner," he muttered. "It's the only way she'll understand."

"I hope you have time for this approach," said Sorrol.

"Varl is right," agreed Matt. "This is the only way to reverse the program—if we can do it at all."

"Shh! Let me continue," implored Varl, turning back to the computer screen. "By opening these valves you will release water at an excessive pressure and speed into the wells."

"Correct," answered the computer.

"Do you have knowledge as to what this program is for?"

"The generation of electricity."

"You have been ill—informed. Your program is to be used for evil means. It has been devised for the destruction of Noxera and all those who live on the surrounding plains. By pumping such a quantity of water into the drilled holes on the fault, a massive buildup of pressure will occur, and an earthquake and tidal wave will follow."

The long eyelashes on the screen fluttered. "I have been built with a conscience. My systems would not allow such a thing to occur."

"You were programmed cleverly so that your knowledge of the pumping process has been built up over years. You know of nothing else but electricity generation, nor would you suspect an alternative motive by your programmers. Am I correct in thinking that your program has been opening valves 1 and 2 for many years?"

"You are correct, but I see no proof in your words. I have also opened valves 3, 6, 4 and 7 recently."

"When have you ever opened *all* of the valves at the same time?" asked Matt, unable to refrain from interrupting.

"Calculate the water pressure and the water flow that you will be sending with all ten valves open. See if I am right," urged Varl. "By my calculations, that amount of water will be demonstrative."

The eyelids closed. Matt and Varl waited patiently. White numbers rolled down the screen in sequences of seven digits.

Matt looked at his watch. "Eighteen minutes left," he

whispered. "This is cutting it mighty close."

"Patience, my boy, have patience."

The computer screen continued to be covered with figures and calculations churning rapidly, scrolling down and across.

Matt tapped his fingers on the console. "Thirteen minutes, Varl—only thirteen minutes left!"

Keela moved closer and stared at the screen with an anxious expression. "Hurry, please," Keela muttered.

The screen suddenly returned to the enormous eyelids. They opened again and the penetrating eyes narrowed into a squint.

"My calculations show that you are correct," the computer said in monosyllabic tone.

Carella gasped.

"Then what you said was true," said Argus.

Matt turned to look at Argus. His face showed utter horror.

"Will you help us, computer?" asked Varl.

The eyes blinked twice. "I will. What do you require of me?"

"You must close down valves 3 through 10 immediately. Valves 1 and 2 must be left open for electricity generation."

"It will take time, but I will do as you request."

"Time is running out," said Matt.

The long eyelashes fluttered as if in thought. "According to my calculations, it will take twelve minutes to reconfigure the program."

"Then begin!" shouted Varl. "You must render the Pompeii program inactive forever and return to running the original electricity generation program. Is that understood?"

"Understood."

The atmosphere in the small room was electric. Matt looked at his watch and felt his stomach sink. They would have less than a minute to spare if the computer managed to deactivate the program in the time promised.

He recalled the words of the rhyme and knew that he and Varl had followed the instructions carefully. They had used the knowledge of Braymar and the Freedom Fighters as suggested. By stopping Nonius Balbus and his evil plan they would surely prevent the rise of a new dictator, and by carefully negotiating with the Keeper they would prevent harm to everyone they loved in Karn. Would destroying the Pompeii program, which was the ticking time-bomb within the Keeper, be enough to win his game and save everyone? Matt clenched his fists tightly. Time was now their only real enemy.

He looked at Varl, who seemed transfixed by the screen with the blinking eyelids. Did Varl have any regrets about landing in Karn with him, he wondered, or was he pleased to be yet again helping an oppressed people find freedom?

Keela had her head bowed. She was muttering some words that Matt didn't understand. Sorrol joined in with her, but kept the vidium directed at Carella and Argus. They had known no other life than the harsh rule of the Noxerans. Matt wondered if they were praying. How would they feel if they were given their freedom?

Carella, poor Carella, Matt thought. Carella had worshipped a leader that was evil beyond belief. He had to come to terms with the part he had played in the terrible plan.

Matt broke from his thoughts and looked at his watch again. "Two minutes left," he muttered. "She's got to do it in time!"

Varl looked up. "Never give up hope."

The ground started to shudder. A deafening roar resonated throughout the room. The vibrations grew worse. Matt's teeth chattered. His chair moved several inches away from the computer. He looked in horror at Varl and then at Keela and Sorrol.

"Earthquake or explosion?" Matt asked nervously.

"Not sure," replied Varl, his chair also moving. "Pray that Braymar just succeeded."

"I know he would not let us down," Keela said, grabbing the back of the chair for support.

"We'll know in a few seconds," said Varl.

Matt knew that beneath Keela's optimism she feared the worst. Had Braymar managed to destroy the pipelines?

Then all went quiet. No one spoke.

The eerie silence was suddenly broken by the voice of the computer. "Pompeii program has been permanently deactivated. All files have been erased from my memory. Electricity generation program has been saved and is continuing. All life-support systems in Karn are functioning normally."

The eyelids blinked twice. Matt swore that the evil he had seen earlier within the cold blue eyes had disappeared. It was almost as if the eyes were smiling at him.

"Thank you, Keeper," said Matt. He sighed with relief. "I'm pleased to see that you have a conscience. You've saved the lives of thousands, and prevented your own destruction."

"You are welcome." The eyes closed, and the computer went back into sleep mode.

Matt felt giddy with happiness as their success sunk in. "Thanks, guys!" he said, jumping from his chair. "We did it with teamwork!" He hugged Keela and then Sorrol.

Keela had tears in her eyes. "It is we who should be thanking you. Our lives will be very different from now on."

Matt turned to Varl. He shook the old man's hand firmly. "Once again it has been a pleasure working with you, sir," he said in a businesslike tone. "I hope that I have many more such opportunities."

Varl pulled a twisted smile at his comment. "I am just pleased that we won the game," he whispered. "However, the celebrations are premature."

"They are?" responded Matt, confused.

"This is *not* over yet," said Varl in a loud voice. He walked quickly to the back of the room where Carella and Argus stood watching.

Keela and Sorrol broke off their conversation. They both looked at Matt. Matt shrugged his shoulders and followed Varl, eager to find out what he had meant.

"Carella, we'll get you medical help immediately," said Varl.

Carella nodded. "Thank you. I am sorry that we were blinded by our loyalty to Balbus."

"Loyalty is honorable," replied Varl. "It is unfortunate that in this case it was misguided. But, you will soon have your chance to make amends."

Carella raised his eyebrows. "Indeed?"

"I suspect that Balbus has computers and monitoring equipment on his submarine. He will realize by now that the computer here did not perform the required task of opening the water valves."

"That is correct," confirmed Carella. He looked down at his arm and winced. "I have no doubt that he will be calling my communicator at any time."

"Ah!" said Varl, unclipping the buzzing object from his belt. "Right on cue. Here's your chance, Carella, to do what is right. No word of what has happened here. As far as you are concerned, the computer malfunctioned." He handed the communicator to Carella.

Carella flicked it open with his good hand. He looked at Varl and nodded. Sorrol pointed the vidium at him. Matt held his breath. Would Carella sound convincing?

"Yes, Princeps . . . I realize that, sir . . . No, there was nothing we could do . . . A malfunction of some kind . . . I'm not a computer specialist, sir . . . As you wish, Princeps." Carella flipped down the lid and handed his communicator back to Varl.

"Well?" asked Varl.

"He's returning with a team of computer specialists," announced Carella.

Keela gasped. "I thought Balbus had gone for good. Now what will we do?"

Matt felt sick. This was not going to be easy. Balbus and his legionaries would be armed. How would they combat the vidiums?

Carella grimaced. "I'm sorry. I really did my best."

Varl nodded. "You did well. I suspected Balbus would

come back. After years of planning, he wouldn't walk away now. He'll see his diabolical scheme through to the bitter end. How much time do we have to prepare, Carella?"

"About three hours."

Sorrol lowered the vidium. "I suggest we get back to Area 1 immediately."

"Agreed," said Varl. "Carella, we'll get you a doctor, but we're going to need information from you and Argus first."

Matt swallowed hard. "What are we going to do?"

"We'll think of something," said Varl, putting his arm around Matt's shoulders. "Strategy and careful planning is the key."

Matt sighed. Just when he thought it was all over, the battle was really beginning.

* * * * *

"Welcome back!" shouted Calute as Varl emerged from the pod chute.

Marcella gripped Varl's right hand firmly between her own. "Thank you so *very* much," she said with genuine warmth. Her eyes twinkled with happiness and her huge smile, which seemed permanently fixed from cheek to cheek, made her appear years younger.

Varl peeled off the airpack. He had no idea how he would break the bad news to them. Matt, Keela and Sorrol were silent. Varl realized that Marcella and Calute had not yet noticed their sorrowful expressions.

Braymar arrived with a pile of warm towels. "Good work, my friends," he said, shaking Varl's hand and then Matt's.

"Likewise," responded Varl, toweling himself down.

Braymar looked to the ground. "Unfortunately, old equipment took the life of one of my team members. One set of explosives detonated early."

Varl nodded. "I'm sorry to hear that, Braymar. We thought we heard two explosions."

"Now that the danger has passed we will take a diving team out there to make an exact assessment of the damage," said Braymar.

Varl took a deep breath. He had to tell them immediately. "I'm afraid you'll have to wait. This is not over yet."

Calute, Marcella and Braymar stared at Varl and then at the others. Their happy expressions quickly evaporated. They looked mystified.

"Not over? What do you mean?" asked Calute.

"Balbus is returning," Keela blurted out.

Calute's golden skin looked distinctly paler.

"How do you know?" asked Marcella, shaking visibly.

"I'll explain on the way back to Area 1," Varl replied.

Sorrol removed his headset and handed it to Braymar. "Send a doctor immediately over to Area 6. Carella has been badly injured. He needs to be treated and brought back here. We may need more information from him."

"Right, let's get to work," said Varl, leading the group down the corridor. "We've a lot to do and less than three hours to do it in!"

Chapter 19

Matt stepped out of the pod chute in Area 6. Targon followed. Both of them had refused to stay behind with Calute and Marcella. Matt removed his headset and peeled off his water gear. Three hours had barely been enough time to prepare. The element of surprise would be in their favor, but Balbus was a formidable enemy. Matt scoured the faces of the group of Freedom Fighters. No one else appeared anxious. His stomach churned.

"Everyone know what to do?" asked Varl. "By now Keela and Sorrol will be in position."

Matt's heart raced as he collected his equipment from the container. Targon did the same, smiling nervously as Braymar handed each of them a tranquilizer gun. Matt could see that Targon was also apprehensive.

"Any questions about how to operate this?" Braymar asked.

Matt shook his head. The gun was used by the Karns to stun marine life for research. He lifted the strap over his head and let the bulky weapon hang by his side.

Targon ran his fingers over the long barrel. He shuddered. "I wouldn't want to be on the receiving end of this," he said, checking that the dart chamber was full.

"True, but I feel better knowing that it will only stun and not kill," said Matt. "I won't worry about aiming it at someone."

"Freedom Fighters, are you ready?" bellowed Braymar. He raised his gun in the air above his head.

"Ready!" rang the reply.

"Then let us defeat Balbus and reclaim Karn for all time!"

Braymar marched the group of thirty-six through the watertight doors that separated Area 6 and Area 7. Matt and Targon followed with Varl. They entered the corridor leading to the main airlock. Braymar ushered them all into a small meeting room on the right. Its door gave a clear view of the airlock.

"Positions, everyone!" called Braymar. He lowered the microphone on his headset below his chin. "Sorrol has just called. The submarine is approaching."

"Are you both okay?" asked Varl, turning to Matt and Targon.

Targon nodded.

"Fine, I'm fine," said Matt. His clammy hands could hardly hold the gun.

"As long as Keela and Sorrol succeed at their end, we stand a good chance," said Varl with renewed optimism.

* * * * *

Keela dived into the murky water. She swam to the bottom, sat on the floor of the airlock and attempted to wait patiently. Her breathing was fast. She felt both nervous and excited. Her job was crucial to the success of the operation. She hoped she had the nerve to carry it through. Many people depended upon her.

Sorrol signaled. The submarine had arrived. The huge airlock doors opened inward. Their metal hinges creaked with strain and age. As they opened wider, a glimmer of light shone through the gap. Keela took her position to the side of one door. She looked across at Sorrol, who was close to the other door.

The lights grew brighter as the submarine approached. The craft positioned itself to enter. Keela remained perfectly still with her back to the wall. *By the time they know what has happened, it will be too late,* she thought. *I can do this!*

The droning noise of engines was deafening. Even as the power was cut and the submarine coasted into dock, there was turbulence in the airlock. Keela felt herself thrown against the walls with the movement of the water. She tried to protect the pack she was carrying. Its contents were vital to the operation. If one of the canisters were damaged, Matt, Targon and the others would be put in greater danger.

The doors closed with a loud bang as the two pieces of metal came together. The water began to drain. Keela surfaced with Sorrol to the rear of the sub. They waited under the enormous propeller for the right moment.

She hoped that Carella had been truthful. The success of their plan depended upon his knowledge of how Balbus operated. If Carella were correct, Balbus would take a group of computer specialists and six armed guards into Area 7. The rest of his legionaries, nearly one hundred, would remain in the submarine and continue with their duties. So far

Carella's assessment had been correct. As only one sub could fit in the airlock at a time, Balbus had returned with one submarine.

The hatch clanged open. Voices echoed in the airlock. The legionaries were leaving the submarine. She could hear Balbus bellowing orders at his men. Thundering feet marched along the metal platform toward the inner airlock door. Keela peered out from under one of the large propeller blades. She counted quickly. Carella was right. No more than a dozen men walked toward the door. The moment they had all gone through into the corridor, she and Sorrol would spring into action.

The airlock door slammed closed. Sorrol waited a few seconds, swam to the platform as fast as he could, and locked the airlock to prevent Balbus and his men from returning to their submarine.

Keela climbed the rear ladder of the vessel. Her heart pounded. She made her way across the top of the submarine toward the open hatch. She dug deep into her pack and removed one of the two silver canisters of sleeping gas. Her fingers trembled. She felt for the small clip on the side and pulled it open. The canister hissed. She leaned over the hatch. Her heart skipped a beat. A tiny cry of panic rose in her throat, but she managed to stifle it. A legionary was climbing the ladder! He was only a few feet from the top. She threw the first canister inside the hatch. It would be another ten seconds before it exploded and she had to get both canisters down the hatch in order to knock out the entire submarine crew. She pulled out the second canister and tugged at the clip. It hissed.

The legionary stuck his head through the opening. He lunged for her foot with one hand while clutching the ladder with the other. Keela tried to shake him free, but he clung to her ankle and attempted to pull her toward him. She kicked at his face with her free foot and then, with one sweeping movement, struck him on the head with the hissing canister. The man was temporarily stunned and retreated inside. She hurled the second canister into the submarine with seconds to spare, and pushed the hatch closed. Heart beating furiously, she counted down . . . three . . . two . . . one. Both canisters should have exploded, unleashing their contents. The crew would be knocked out for several hours.

Her heart was still racing when Sorrol appeared. He sprayed sealant around the hatch and sat down next to her.

"Great going," he whispered. "I've contacted Braymar. Now it's up to them."

* * * * *

Matt peered through the crack in the door. He heard voices. Balbus and his men were approaching. With Keela and Sorrol's success their chances had increased. The Princeps would be cornered and would not be able to call for reinforcements. Matt gulped. There was no turning back.

Varl held up his fingers and counted down. "Here we go," he said, striding into the corridor. Matt stepped after him, closely followed by Targon. They stood on either side of Varl and aimed the silvery shafts of their tranquilizer guns at the enemy.

Balbus looked bewildered. Then he smiled and stepped

forward to within inches of Varl's weapon. "Senator Varl, young Marcus and one other, I presume."

"Indeed," replied Varl.

Balbus chuckled and thrust his right hand in the air. "Legionaries, do not draw your vidiums."

"A sensible order, Princeps. But now you will surrender," said Varl, as if it were the natural thing for Balbus to do.

Balbus folded his hands across his plump belly and howled with laughter. "I *really* feel threatened!" he joked. He reached forward and tapped the end of Varl's tranquilizer gun as if it were a toy.

Braymar and the freedom fighters filed out of the room and lined up across the corridor in rows behind Varl. They raised their guns. The expression on Balbus' face changed instantly. His smile disappeared and his eyes bulged with anger.

"Still you are no threat," he sneered. "A small group of men with outdated weaponry. What match are you for a force such as mine? You fail to realize I have another hundred men at my immediate disposal."

Varl smiled. "You arrogant man! Try and call them!"

Balbus pulled out his communicator and flipped it open. He hesitated as if he expected to be fired upon. When no one moved, he punched two buttons. His cheek twitched under his left eye and he blinked furiously while he waited for a response. There was none. He lowered the communicator slowly. His eyes narrowed. He glowered at Varl.

"So, it appears you have blocked my communication system somehow," he snorted. "This feeble party is still no match for my legionaries. Odds are, you will be slaughtered."

It was Varl's turn to laugh. "I am a scientist. I do not gamble. Do the math! You have six unarmed computer specialists and six armed guards. We outnumber you three to one."

Matt smiled. Balbus' twitch worsened by the minute. He shook his head quickly from side to side, obviously under pressure. Matt stood tall and kept his finger firmly on the trigger.

"How do you know about my computer specialists?" Balbus opened his mouth wide with horror and screamed, "Carella has betrayed me!"

The computer specialists moved to one side. Balbus' legionaries spread across the width of the corridor and raised their vidiums.

"Yes, Balbus. Carella and Argus saw sense. They learned what you had in store for their families." Varl pointed to Matt. "This young man knows a great deal about computers. We overrode your Pompeii program. Men will stand up and die, rather than see an evil tyrant such as you kill thousands of innocent people."

"Kill them!" shouted Balbus. "Kill them all!"

"Hold your fire or Balbus dies!" screamed Varl, as the legionaries took aim. "My gun is aimed directly at your Princeps. You fire on us and he's a dead man."

The legionaries looked at each other, confused by the conflicting orders. One by one they lowered their vidiums. Matt's heart slowed but he kept a tight hold on the gun.

"Kick the vidiums over here," ordered Varl.

"No!" Balbus yelled. His faced twitched uncontrollably. "Fire, I tell you, fire!"

One of the guards took aim at Varl. Braymar saw the movement and without hesitation shot him in the shoulder. The guard fell to the floor, seemingly dead.

Balbus' cheeks bulged and the blood vessels in his neck pulsed visibly.

"Destroy them!" he bellowed.

Balbus clutched his chest. His face turned purple. He wheezed and choked, reaching for Varl's arms, grabbing Varl's clothing as he crashed to the floor. Several legionaries started to move forward to help their leader.

"Get back!" shouted Braymar, thrusting his weapon at them. "No one move!"

Matt stared in horror. "What's happening?"

Varl dropped his gun and tried to loosen the cloak from around the Princeps' neck. "I think he's having a heart attack. Get a doctor!"

Balbus' eyes grew wide. He raised his arms in a sudden movement and with both hands gripped Varl around the neck.

Varl fought for breath. He began to suffocate. He tried to pull the strong fingers away from his throat.

"Die!" Balbus gasped.

Matt rushed to Varl's aid. He tugged at the Princeps' arms, digging his nails into the man's fleshy wrists. Balbus let out one long breath. His arms relaxed and then dropped to his side. His chest failed to rise again. He lay motionless on the floor.

Varl sat beside the body and took several deep breaths. He was white with the shock of Balbus' attempt on his life.

"Is he dead?" asked Targon, his voice shaking.

"I think so," replied Varl quietly. He rubbed his neck and struggled to his feet.

Matt looked again at Balbus. The man's eyes stared hauntingly at him. Although Matt hated to see anyone suffer such a death, he felt nothing but relief. With Balbus gone, the fear he had spread also disappeared. In life he had terrorized so many. In death he appeared a harmless, feeble old man.

Varl gripped Matt's arm and led him away from the body. Matt stood in a daze watching the rest of the proceedings.

Braymar ordered his men to cuff the legionaries and then used his communicator to call Sorrol and Calute. One of the Freedom Fighters placed a blanket over Nonius Balbus.

Sorrol and Keela came running down the corridor.

"Thank you, my friends," said Sorrol, panting. He shook Varl's hand with fervor.

Keela's face was radiant. "It is *finally* over!" she said excitedly.

"And thank you both for a job well done," replied Varl. "The ending was not quite as we had visualized, but at least no blood was shed."

Keela looked at the covered body. "There are few who will feel sorry for him," she said coldly. "I still do not understand how someone can have such little respect for human life."

"All for power," mumbled Matt.

Braymar joined the conversation. "Carella and Argus have arranged for Noxeran help to take the submarine back to the mainland. All of Balbus' men will stand trial. Carella and Argus will be treated leniently after the help they gave today." He smiled. "I assure you Karn will be ruled wisely and fairly. Freedom is very valuable, and it will not be taken lightly."

Varl nodded. "We couldn't agree more."

"Marcella and Calute want you to join us for a celebratory banquet," said Keela excitedly.

"That'll be great," said Matt.

Targon grinned. "I'm quite hungry, now that you mention it."

"I think we'll need to freshen up first," said Varl. He put one arm around Matt and the other around Targon. "Let's go back to our suite."

"I believe that your friend, Dorin, is waiting for you," Braymar called after them. "He has made a fine recovery, but still needs rest and care. I am sure that he will be happy to know that you are safe."

"It will be nice for the four of us to be together," added Varl.

" . . . *And* important," stressed Matt.

Varl gave him a sideways glance. "Indeed."

Epilogue

Varl returned from his bathroom wearing the long white robe in which he had arrived in Karn.

Matt smiled. "It's good to see you back in your regular clothing."

"Likewise," responded Varl, taking a seat next to Dorin on the sofa in the living area. "You look like Matt again. I never really liked the Karn tunics!"

"Now you tell us!" quipped Targon.

Matt sat on the floor next to his friend and opened up his laptop. He sighed. "Are you ready for this?"

They nodded in agreement. He began to type in the commands to end the final scenario. Varl leaned forward to watch over Targon's shoulder. Dorin held his breath.

A familiar greeting flashed up on the screen. Matt smiled with relief.

"What does it say? Tell us," said Targon eagerly.

"It says: Congratulations! You have successfully completed Level 2, Keeper of the Realm. Press *'Enter'* to continue."

"Great!" said Targon, slapping Matt's hand in a gesture of 'high five.' "I knew we'd win!"

"Well, what are you waiting for?" asked Varl, prodding Matt in the back to urge him on. "Press the key, and let's all get back to where we should be."

"Yeah, I'm ready to go home," agreed Matt, his finger

hovering over the word '*Enter.*' "I've had enough adventure to last me the rest of my life." He pressed the key quickly and watched as the new instructions appeared on the screen.

Matt's happy expression turned to one of dismay as he digested the words before him. He couldn't believe what he read on the screen. Varl was silent.

"What is it?" demanded Targon, shaking Matt's shoulders. "Why are you both quiet? Has the battery gone dead? Someone read it to me, *please.*"

Matt gulped. His voice quivered as he read, "Welcome to Level 3, *Keeper of the Empire*. This is your most dangerous challenge yet. Do you accept the mission? Press '*Enter*' to continue." He looked at Varl with saucer-shaped eyes that conveyed his mixed emotions.

Varl stared back, his face pale. "The third level, eh?"

Dorin used the arm of the sofa to hobble to his feet. "I'm sorry, but I must say good-bye to you all and leave the room. I am too old, and in no condition for another dangerous mission."

Matt scrambled off the floor and hugged him tightly. "What will you do?"

"Don't you worry about me—I'll be just fine. I quite like it here. I'm treated well, and Karn is now free of the Noxerans. There is nothing back in Zaul that can't wait."

"But how will you get back?" asked Targon, tears welling in his eyes.

"If you can come back for me, or, if I should find my way back to Zaul, so be it," said Dorin, ruffling his hair. "If not, I will be fine living out my days here."

Varl shook Dorin's hand and embraced him tightly.

"Good luck, my friend. We'll really miss you."

"And I'll miss you," he said, as he moved slowly across the room. He paused at the door. "Beat Level 3 for me!"

Matt, Varl and Targon sat down on the floor around the laptop in silence and sadness. They each held onto the computer screen tightly.

"Are we ready, then?" Matt asked quietly.

"Ready," they agreed.

Matt pressed '*Enter.*'

Also by H.J. Ralles

Keeper of the Kingdom

ISBN 1-929976-03-8
Top Publications January 2001

In 2540 AD, the Kingdom of Zaul is an inhospitable world controlled by Cybergon 'Protectors' and ruled by 'The Keeper'. Humans are 'Worker' slaves, eliminated without thought. Thank goodness this is just a computer game—or is it? For Matt, the Kingdom of Zaul becomes all too real when his computer jams and he is sucked into the game. Now he is trapped, hunted by the Protectors and hiding among the Workers to survive. Matt must use his knowledge of computers and technology to free the people of Zaul and return to his own world. *Keeper of the Kingdom* is a gripping tale of technology out of control.

Darok 9

ISBN 1-929976-10-0
Top Publications January 2002

In 2120 AD, the barren surface of the moon is the only home that three generations of earth's survivors have ever known. Towns, called Daroks, protect inhabitants from the extreme lunar temperatures. But life is harsh. Hank Havard, a young scientist is secretly perfecting SH33, a drug that eliminates the body's need for water. When his First Quadrant laboratory is attacked, Hank saves his research onto memory card and runs from the enemy. Aided by Will, his teenage nephew, and Maddie, Will's computer-literate classmate, Hank must conceal SH33 from the dreaded Fourth Quadrant. But suddenly Will's life is in danger. Who can Hank trust—and is the enemy really closer to home?

The Keeper Series Continues . . .

Keeper of the Empire

The Vorgs have landed! They're grotesque, they spit venom and Matt is about to be their next victim. What are these lizard-like creatures doing in Gova? Why are humans wandering around like zombies? In the third book of the Keeper series, Matt finds himself in a terrifying world. With the help of his friend Targon, and a daring girl named Angel, Matt must locate the secret hideout of the Govan Resistance. And what has become of the wise old scientist, Varl? There is no end to the action and excitement as Matt attempts to track down the Keeper, and win the next level of his computer game.

To be released 2004

H.J. Ralles

H. J. Ralles lives in Dallas, Texas with her husband, two teenage sons and a devoted black Labrador. *Keeper of the Realm* is her third novel.

Visit H.J. Ralles at her website

www.hjralles.com